INHERIT THE STARS

Tessa Elwood

RP | TEENS
PHILADELPHIA · LONDON

Books published by Running Press are available at special discounts for
bulk purchases in the United States by corporations, institutions, and
other organizations. For more information, please contact the Special
Markets Department at the Perseus Books Group, 2300 Chestnut
Street, Suite 200, Philadelphia, PA 19103, or call (800) 810-4145, ext.
5000, or e-mail special.markets@perseusbooks.com.

ISBN 978-0-7624-5840-0

Library of Congress Control Number: 2015934958

E-book ISBN 978-0-7624-5841-7

9 8 7 6 5 4 3 2
Digit on the right indicates the number of this printing

Designed by Frances J. Soo Ping Chow
Edited by Lisa Cheng
Typography: Lato and Mercury

Published by Running Press Teens
An Imprint of Running Press Book Publishers
A Member of the Perseus Books Group
2300 Chestnut Street
Philadelphia, PA 19103–4371

Visit us on the web!
www.runningpress.com/rpkids

To that Chrystal,
because it's her favorite.

And to my family and loved ones,
who endlessly inspire.

THE
BLIGHT

BOMBS HAVE NICKNAMES. INNOCUOUS, HAPPY nicknames. The thundering yellow cloud licking our flightwing's windows has got to be a Baby Sunshine.

"M'lady?!" screams the pilot from the open cockpit. "M'lady are you—"

The flightwing bucks and Wren's medibed wrenches from the hook I've only half fastened, and skids across the cargo bay. I slam into the wall a second before she does. The bed rams my stomach—pressure and pain and ripping corners and oh God I'm going to die.

And so will Wren, if we don't reach the specialist.

"Go!" I yell. "Go, go, *go.*"

The flightwing banks, and I grab the bed rail so my sister doesn't fly across the hold.

Wren's makeshift bandage is red and there's so much blood on her face I can't tell if it's dripping and my palms sweat fire and her bed wants to roll away.

"I've got you," I say. "I've got you, I've got—"

Something booms, and I'd give anything to reach the window—but anything means letting go of Wren.

The wing rolls and we both pitch forward, bed wheels screeching murder. I scramble across the slick metal floor, flailing against the wall for something. Anything. My fingers brush one of the yellow safety straps, and I latch on. Wren keeps rolling but I have her. Won't let go.

My arm's going to split its socket.

The pilot swears, the wing swings near vertical, and Wren slams my stomach through my spine.

But her head's close enough to see now, and her bandage *is* dripping. A lot.

She's going to die before we get out of the city airspace, let alone off-planet to the moon station's medic specialist.

"You're all right." I let go of the safety strap long enough to pat her cheek—the nonbroken bits. "Wren? Wren, look at me. You're all right. I promise."

She doesn't respond. She hasn't responded since the last bomb hit and she pulled me through the riot. She'd gone out to stand with her soldiers. Because that's what a Base Commander does. Fights for her people.

Even if they're the ones bombing her.

Another booming ricochet, but this time the flightwing is level and doesn't rock.

The window is three steps away—high, round, and trimmed white. I glance at Wren, but her eyelashes don't move. I rub the sweat from one palm, switch my hands on the rail, and repeat with the other. Then I inch us toward the window.

One step, two, and—

The city stretches below, blue and gold, sleek skytowers and open streets. Explosive yellow answered by streaked neon pink.

Pink? The Kiss Pop bombs? But the city gangs don't have those. When they raided the armory, the gangs only took the Sunshines and some sparkguns. Wren double-checked the base inventory like ten times. Nothing else was stolen.

Which means our soldiers are retaliating, throwing Kiss Pops to fight the Sunshines. As if the city gangs are some kind of invading force, not desperate civilians.

Of course the gangs attacked the base. They thought we had food.

I pull the bed close and reach for Wren's wrist, find the communicator watch she usually issues commands through. Except the screen is busted and won't light up no matter how hard I tap.

"Okay," I say. "Okay. Where's your flipcom?" I skim through all Wren's pockets. "Come on, you always have it."

She does. Even now, broken and bloody.

And alive. Absolutely, positively alive.

I pull the flipcom from her jacket, and press the fast-connect circle on the neon screen.

"Connecting," says the male automation. "Please, wait."

The flightwing slowly inclines; Wren's bed shifts as we gain height. I dig my heels into the floor.

"Connecting, please—"

"My Lady?" Casser booms, thick with astonishment and hope.

"You have to stop firing!" I say.

Screams in the background, crashes and static.

"Asa?" Casser asks.

"You have to stop, they're our people!"

"The gangs? They're bombing *us*."

"Because they're *hungry*. They think all the stockpiled food is safe! Do not fire!"

Except hungry isn't the right word. Not after seven months quarantined on a Blighted planet, where everything is contaminated, even us. Wren's endless ration cuts couldn't stretch the supplies out forever.

Not that the city knows that because Wren told the cameras we had enough food, more than enough to get through. Showed off the packed supply warehouse in light bright enough to hide the food's tainted green glow. I'd confronted her after the cameras left, and she rounded on me. *What would you have me say?* she asked. *We're all going to starve?*

In the speakers, someone calls Casser's name and he barks a muffled order.

"Asa. This is an emergency state, we cannot allow civilians to—"

"No! No retaliation. They're our people. We protect *them*. You know what Dad always says—"

"My Lord isn't here and neither are you." Sharp in the speakers, sharper under my skin. "I know you're worried for your sister, but I don't have time for this."

"Captain Casser." I put Dad in my voice and steel in my spine. "You will regain the parameter and minimize damage, but you will not retaliate. You will protect our people— *all* our people—on the base and off."

Restrained, silent thunder.

I may be youngest—sixteen to Wren's twenty, and not firstborn Heir and future ruler of our interplanetary House, but I'm still a Daughter of Fane. Dad can gainsay me.

The captain can't.

"Do. Not. Fire," I say.

"As you say, my lady," he barks and hangs up.

AS SOON AS WE LAND ON THE MOON STATION, I OPEN the rear hold as the pilot scrambles out of the cockpit. He pushes while I pull, and Wren's medibed bumps down the flightwing's ramp. Her body jerks with the wheels. Her head bounces. The pilot's grip slides off the rail and the bed skitters toward the hard metal dock.

"Hold on!" I shout, but I can't manage it either—the bed's too heavy and my hands are too slick. I swing around the end. Wren's boots jam my stomach and my heels skid, but the bed stops. I glare up the ramp. "You have to hold on!"

The pilot wants to crawl out of his skin. I swear I can see nail scratches under his cheeks.

"I'm sorry, My Lady." He lowers his head, voice barely a whisper, emphasizing the capitals as if addressing Wren.

Or worse, Dad.

"No, I didn't mean that!" I reach toward him, but my foot slips and the bed with me. I lock my legs. "You're fine, she's fine, everything's fine. Okay? We're *fine.*"

The pilot stares at the floor and doesn't answer.

"I promise." I look between Wren's bloodied face to his bloodless one. "We're going to be all right." The words crack and the pilot looks up.

Wren doesn't.

"M'lady? M'lady Asa?!" An older man with hair as white as Casser's runs across the dim metal docking bay, thin arms pumping above scissor legs. He stops at the ramp's edge, eyeing the bright white and brown armband that identifies me as Dad's. He grabs the bed rails, takes some of the weight. Three half moons and a star hover over the breast pocket of his uniform, which makes him the moon station commander. "You're finally leaving quarantine? My Lady Wren finally convinced you? My Lord *will* be pleased."

Dad wanted Wren to ship me to our home planet, Malsa, as soon as Urnath had to be quarantined. Wren was needed, in charge of Urnath and its people. I was just visiting for the summer.

As if I'd let Wren face the Blight alone.

"I'll contact Lord Fane as soon as the communicator's up," the commander says.

"It's down?" I ask.

"Only since yesterday, m'lady." The station commander helps me navigate the medibed down the ramp. "Don't worry, we'll get it working. Now, who's this?"

He flips the bandage away from Wren's uniform insignia. Six crescents between two full moons, representing our twenty-six planets. The official House of Fane crest.

The commander snatches his hand away and fists it to his heart. "My Lady."

"The specialist," I say. "Medic Sansa, where is she?"

"She completed Decontamination yesterday. Left with

the evacuation transport to Malsa this morning."

"No, she can't have. She's here, I know she's here. I watched Wren sign her quarantine release to this station a couple of weeks ago!"

"Five weeks, m'lady." He won't meet my eyes.

Decontamination only takes four.

Time blurs in quarantine, especially when it goes on months and months, but I should have remembered. Paid attention, wrote it down.

"Then—" But it's barely a word. I try again. "Then we need whoever you have."

He just looks at me.

"You have someone? You have to have someone."

He shakes his head and doesn't stop. "We only have the medic techs, m'lady. None qualified for this. We don't have the facilities anymore, everything's been remapped for Decontamination processing." He turns to the pilot. "Can you—?"

The pilot's face answers for him. We don't have fuel to return to Urnath. We barely had fuel enough to make it here. Energy is precious and was under ration long before quarantine and the Blight.

I told the pilot to fly us to the moon station. Medic Sansa is the best, House-renown. The city is under riot, but it is safe here. No street gangs. Wren should have been fine by now, the specialist already operating.

I've just killed my sister.

And they know it, the station commander and the pilot. Wide eyes fixed on me for the solution, as if I have all the answers. As if I can magically knit together the gullies in Wren's scalp. As if I can fix everything.

As if I'm Dad.

"Stitches. She needs stitches. And the blood cleaned off. And probably a fluid tube. And get the communicator up, I need to talk to Dad."

THE SHOWER PELTS MY NECK IN ICE. HEAT REQUIRES energy, and whatever heat there was left ten minutes ago.

I can't tell what's colder, the water or me. I hug my chest and sway, but my arms are coldest of all.

"M'lady?" calls a woman through the closed shower stall. One of the moon station soldiers. Chelsey? Kelena? "M'lady, are you all right?"

"F-fine." My hair is in my mouth, stuck to my tongue. I suck the water off.

They're going to shave my head. They already shaved Wren's. Sliced away her blonde curls, crusted red. They wouldn't let me save even one. Too hard to decontaminate.

"Are you sure, m'lady?"

"Yes."

My hair tastes gritty and metallic, like pavement and smoke. Street kids in bandannas, screaming, *you can't starve us forever!*

Or maybe, *Asa! Get your hair out of your mouth. You're not two.*

Or maybe that's Wren.

They've probably stitched her up by now. That's what they said they would do.

I sink down to my toes, fingertips spread on the floor. The water gnaws.

"M'lady, the initial treatment starts soon, for Decontamination? You said you wanted to be processed as soon as possible? So we can get you and my Lady home?"

I don't move. The cold is nice. Ices over the gaps.

Get up.

I raise my head and can almost see her. Wren. Tiny fists to match her toothy lisp, back when she was taller than me. *You get up. We're Fane and everybody's looking, so you get* up.

But I didn't. I was three and thought Mom's leaving was the worst thing in the world.

I was wrong.

"M'lady, are you—"

"Here." I push off the floor and deactivate the water. "I'm here."

THE LONG MIRROR REFLECTS A MULTICOLORED ARMY OF bald stick figures, and I can't tell which one is me. Wren would know, but she's getting her head stitched six floors above.

"Cover your faces, please," calls the intercom.

We do, all ten of us, arms tucked against our chests. We're in bras and shorts and nothing else, not even shoes. My feet stick to the floor. The Decontamination rooms are makeshift at best, and all of Urnath has to be evacuated through this station.

"Don't let it in your mouth," says the girl next to me. "You'll never get it out."

I squeeze my lips tight.

"Ready? First dusting in three, two—"

Soft pops overhead. Airy powder pillows my skin, burrows through my pores like painless acid. An ashen residue that whispers corrosion.

"Turn, please," says the intercom. "Second dusting in three, two, one."

More pops and pillows. More breezy powder that doesn't quite hurt.

We turn three more times. Then a solder enters in a white, full-body Decontamination suit and ushers us into the Fan Room, where they try to blow our skin away. After that comes new clothes, with round trash bins for the old ones, and then freedom.

We walk spaced out and sticking together through the narrow corridor of silver walls and safety lights. The hall is cold and growing colder. The new fuel factories were supposed to fix that—the cold, the entire energy crisis—and create a safe, sustainable replacement for uleum, the current universal energy standard. Uleum is finite and almost gone.

"Your first time?" asks the girl from the powder room. She glistens sallow, and her loose shirt sticks tight to her ribs as she pulls on her jacket. I can count the bones under her skin.

I nod. "You?"

"Fifteenth. Bad enough Fane poisoned the planet, now he de-poisons us every damn day."

"He didn't mean to."

"God, you think?" She kicks at the floor. "I don't know anymore."

"I do." I sink into my jacket, but it doesn't help. "He wouldn't have built the factories, if he'd known they'd cause the Blight. He'd have found another way."

She snorts. "Riiiight, and I'm sure you have that on first-hand authority."

"Yes."

The girl sighs at the ceiling. "Listen, sweetie, you—" Then she looks at me. Really looks, past the clothes and my hairless scalp. Her voice rises. "Lady Asa?"

Every footstep stops. The women ahead look over their shoulders, the girls behind sink into their coats, and I am in a bubble alone.

"He shut the factories down." I look between them, all of them, gaunt cheeks and tired eyes. "As soon as he knew about the Blight. The new fuel was everything he ever worked for, and as soon as he knew, he stopped production. Didn't even hesitate. That's how I know."

"LADY ASA?"

"Wren?" I jerk upright and blink the medibed into focus as I slide off the chair to kneel at her side. She lies freshly stitched and stable, while Urnath looms through the window-wall beyond—clouded yellow like a small, sickly sun. The commander converted one of the moon station offices for us so we could have our own room, away from everyone else. I slip my fingers through Wren's and hold tight. "I'm here, it's okay, I'm right here."

She doesn't squeeze back. Her hand is limp.

Behind me, someone coughs. An I'd-rather-be-anywhere-else cough. Reality wavers, cracked as hard as Wren's skull.

Wren would never call me Lady.

I curl into the bed frame.

"Um, m'lady? We got the communicator up?" High and hesitant and nothing like Wren.

I've forgotten what she sounds like already.

No. Don't cry. Fane doesn't cry.

Wren didn't when Dad put us under quarantine, or when the months dragged on and the riots started. Not even when she stood on a makeshift podium and told an entire population they'd have to evacuate their home planet. That Urnath's once abundant fields could no longer grow food or maintain life. That they never would again.

"M'lady?"

19

"Dad." I sit back on my heels and brace my hands on the mattress's edge. "Did you get Dad?"

"Yes, m'lady. Our visual communicator's broken, so we channeled it to a flipcom." A bony hand slips into my peripheral, lays a battered flipcom onto the bed. "I hope that's all right."

I snatch it up. "Yes, perfect, thank you."

"Do you need anything else, m'lady?"

"No, thank you." *Go away.*

Maybe the last wasn't just in my head. Her footsteps speed across the carpet and the door clicks shut.

I press the com to my ear. "Dad?"

"You do not give my men orders under any circumstances," says the speaker, spring-loaded and deadly soft. "But especially not in a state of emergency with the base under attack."

Him. Wholly, absolutely. It's all I can do not to cry. "Oh, Dad."

"You restricted Casser's ability to handle an emergency situation, and that is unacceptable." Softer still and *him.*

I collapse into the bedside. "When will you be here? Wren won't wake up."

"I asked you a question, Asa."

"I thought the specialist was here but she's not, and nobody else knows how to fix her, and we don't have enough fuel to go back planet-side and I thought she'd be safe here but she's not and Dad I'm so sorry but you have to—"

"Asa!" explodes through the speakers. "You will never issue another thoughtless command I cannot easily repeal without undermining the authority of this House. Is that *clear*?"

Commands. Telling Casser not to retaliate. Ordering the pilot to fly Wren here. My fault.

Mine mine mine.

"Yes, sir," I say.

"This doesn't happen again." Not quite an order, just almost.

"No, sir."

"I have your word?"

"Yes, sir."

Something pings on his end. A rustle of fabric, the click of buttons. He's probably checking another communications screen.

"Good," he says, and I don't know if it's for me or whoever else is there. "I'll call again next week. If you need to reach me before then, I've given the outpost captain my direct line."

I can almost feel him hanging up. "Dad, wait!"

"Yes?"

"When will you get us? When will you be here?"

"You can't come home yet, Asa."

I clutch the blanket for support. Which is stupid, because I'm already on the floor.

No, of course I can't. He doesn't *need* to take me, too.

"Wren," I say. "Not me. When are you getting Wren?"

"No one leaves quarantine still contaminated." Absolute, without recourse. "No one."

"But there's no equipment here or specialists and they can't even scan her head to see what's wrong and she hasn't woken up, not once, and—"

"She's fine, the medichip will keep her stabilized until Decontamination's complete."

He doesn't know?

Right, because after removing an implanted, priceless biotech chip that's supposed to heal anything up to and probably including death, the first thing Wren would do is tell Dad.

Especially after swearing to skin me if I ever opened my mouth.

I straighten. "No, Dad, Wren isn't chipped."

"What?"

"She took it out."

"Took it out," he repeats.

"When the base was running out of uleum. Really running out, Dad, not just low rations, and we didn't have

22

any food, either. All the nearby farms were Blighted and we had to ship food in from places it hadn't reached yet. Except the only fuel we had was ecoflux, from the factories before you shut them down, and Wren thought if we could just get the old flightwings to run on the new energy, it'd solve everything."

"Asa."

"And she needed to take the medichip apart because, well, Wren could explain it, but it works by making the body think all the fake biotech cells are actual *cell* cells, because of some kind of signal they give off? She thought if she could just duplicate that—"

"*Enough*, Asa. Now is *not* the time. If you want to manipulate me, find a lie I cannot directly contradict," he says with the special, controlled evisceration reserved for me alone.

"I'm not—" I try to sniff back the tears, but it just makes it worse. "Mom."

"What?"

I'm not *her*.

Or maybe I am. I just killed Wren.

"Lying. I'm not lying."

"That is *not* what you said."

"Please. Dad." I space the words, keep them even. "Wren isn't chipped. There's nobody here to help. I'll stay here forever if it makes you happy, but you have to get Wren. It's not her fault I brought her up here, Dad *please.*"

"Silence.

"There's too much at stake," he says at last, "after Decontamination I will personally come pick you up. It's not forever, you can survive a month."

"Wren can't."

"Enough."

"She'll *die.*"

"Asa."

"You have to—"

"No." Final. Dad final.

"Then don't come for us at all," I say and disconnect.

I drop the com and scoot back along the carpet, away from the dull screen and mute speaker. The black hole sucking out Wren's life and my soul.

I hung up on Dad.

No one hangs up on Dad.

"Wren?"

She doesn't answer. The light festers over her gaunt cheeks. I run both of my hands through my hair.

Except I don't have any.

I hold my breath until I'm light-headed and swaying, but I don't cry.

I don't.

"I'm here." I move to the bed and slide my hand under

hers. Our palms match, same size, same fingers—except hers always know what to do. "It's okay, I swear it's okay. I've got you. I'm sorry, I'm so sorry. Wren? Wren, please. Wake up."

LOSS

"ALL INNOVATIONS TAKE TIME." DAD LEANS over the podium, his amplified voice bouncing off skytowers and the gathered crowd. Thousands. So many they're almost a texture—packing the square, the streets of Malsa. Oval Park holds the capital's heartbeat, the grassy eye amid a hurricane of towers, thoroughfares, and people.

So many people.

We stand on a round dais erected for the occasion, simple and high so we are visible from all directions. Dad and Emmie and me.

But not Wren.

It's been six months and she hasn't woken once.

"The best innovations take trial and error. Despite the setbacks of its initial manufacture, ecoflux *is* our best innovation." Dad rechanneled the skytower ad-screens, and every last one reflects his face. "As terrifying as the Blight was, it has been contained and eliminated. Ecoflux itself was always safe. Now its manufacture will be as well."

The screens switch from Dad to the rebuilt factories, surrounded by trees bursting with un-Blighted life. The factories' rising gray cylinders are backed by blue sky and stamped with the ecoflux logo—a rectangular uleum ration token that dissipates into a bird's wing. Flight and freedom and infinite resource. A new fuel that will never require rationing because we don't have to extract it from a planet's core.

Wren's design.

Dad's voice deepens, reverberates. "We have nothing to fear and everything to gain."

The crowd shuffles uneasy feet.

It's easy to gain everything when "everything" was lost. Urnath's dead, the whole planet evacuated and abandoned. The Blighted areas on our other planets—ten total, infected by prequarantine travelers—are contained but forever unlivable. Choked, dusty landscapes where nothing grows.

We'll never get them back.

Emmie bumps my shoulder. Daggers shoot from underneath her long lashes, her heels high enough she doesn't have to crane her neck to face me. Of the three of us, she's the closest to Dad—short with his sharp angles and a heart-stopping smile. Wren took his undercurrents, his poise and motion. I only got his hands.

"Smile," says Emmie. "This is not your deathbed."

I straighten. Smile into upturned faces. Our dais afloat in a peopled sea.

Sunlight fractures off Dad's signet ring as he waves to our left, at the one street lined with hoverbuses instead of people. The city's new public transit system, neon and gleaming and powered by ecoflux.

"Starting today, production of all uleum fueled engines and power grids will discontinue to make way for the future. Our future. Free of blackouts and ration tokens, of monthly fuel allotments drawn from depleting reserves. Never again will you have to choose between heating your homes or powering your flightwings. Never again will we strip and gut a planet in our system for our uleum mines. We have lost Urnath, but how many planets have we *intentionally* wasted just to have another few decades of fuel?"

Four. Four unpopulated planets carefully stripped, mined, and rationed.

"Oh, well played, Dad," Emmie says, long hair falling over her shoulder to brush silk against mine. "Nothing like a little guilt to grease the gears."

His voice rises until the platform vibrates power. "Ecoflux is a stable, *sustainable* energy. This is the day history will talk about. This is the day we change our fate. And to honor that future, my youngest has requested a few words."

Only if requested means ordered.

I bury my hands in my skirt.

Dad steps away from the podium, dragging a House-worth of stares to fixate on me—my hair. Or lack thereof. At least my scalp doesn't show anymore. Mostly. My proof that I was *there*. Was evacuated, decontaminated, and processed like everyone else.

I am proof the House of Fane understands.

No one trusts the new energy, Dad had said. *Make them.*

Wren could. She'd look out with all Dad's power and transform sunlight into stories—and then make them true. She wouldn't take no for an answer, not from the crowd, not even from Dad.

But I did. Wren would be awake right now if I hadn't. The medicenter specialist said as much. That each untreated day in Decontamination lessened her chances. Once we were home, Dad had Wren scanned for a medichip. Three times. And then he punched an empty wall.

"Sometime this year." Emmie slips a hand behind my back and presses me forward. My palms find the podium's sleek steel curves. Between them, the embedded prompt screen glows with everything I have to say. Dad's words, his speech.

It's short. All I have to do is read.

When Father told me about the new transit system, the text reads.

I can do this. I can.

"When Dad told—"

The screen flashes bright red and I freeze.

Father, blinks the text. *Father*.

Everyone's watching. Our entire House.

"When Father said—"

The screen flashes.

"Told, when he told, when *Father* told me that—"

Red red red.

"That—about—"

"Asa," mutters Dad, a three-letter oath.

"I'm not *Wren*," I say under my breath, but the speaker doesn't understand whispers. It throws mine everywhere.

Faces. Unrelenting silence and craning necks. Behind me, Emmie swears.

Dad has no expression at all.

Don't cry. Absolutely do *not* cry.

"I'm not Wren." I press both hands flat against the podium, cover the screen's red punctuation. "And she would know what to say because she loved ecoflux. Helped Dad develop it. I mean, you remember, right? That big opening ceremony? How excited she was?" I scan the crowd for post shaved heads, the easiest Decontamination marker from far away. The colors blur, but there are two women in front of me, farther out, and an older man near the platform's edge to my left. "Ecoflux is like—it's like kinetic hope. The kind that lives outside your head. A touchable freedom. No more rations. We can go anywhere, power anything, which was what all this was for. It has to be worth it." I point at the shiny new hoverbuses. "We make it worth it."

I push away from the podium. Dad blocks the way to the stairs. I swing left, toward the man with the bone-tight cheeks, and crouch on the dais edge. "Help me down? I need to ride the bus."

He reaches up without hesitation, and I'm on my feet on the ground before I can even push off to help. His forehead is a network of age and worry, his eyes an odd gray white that doesn't match his skin.

Decontamination does that sometimes.

I tap the edge of my own eye. "Did your toenails fall off, too?"

His lips catch between a phrase or three, before breaking into a smile. "No, but my daughter's did."

He steps back and lets go, the crowd opening a little to give us room.

"Have hers grown back? Because Aston at the medicenter on South has this stuff that kind of works? Well, it hasn't yet, but he promises—"

The hard thump of landing feet, and suddenly everyone in our tiny circle is five steps away, heads half-bowed.

Dad's radiation scalds my neck.

The man backs up. "My Lord."

Dad nods acknowledgment as his fingers dig into my back and march me forward. The crowd parts in waves.

I look over my shoulder. "Aston on South. Tell him I sent you."

Dad's arm tightens, but he nods to the man in confirmation. Wren or not, I'm a Daughter of Fane.

And everyone is watching.

WREN'S SCALP IS A PALE MASS OF STARBURSTS INSTEAD of angry rifts. They give her baby face a new dimension, a tough don't-mess-with-me quality at odds with her round nose and mouth. We sit propped against the pillows like always, while her bedside monitor beeps through a mountainscape of multicolored lines. Birds jostle their bright window feeder with a tangle of chirps and wing beats. Sunlight catches the tips of their wings and the myriad skytowers beyond—all white and brown today. House Colors in celebration of the transit system. Tomorrow they'll reprogram the colorbot siding and return the towers to the normal blue or green or gray.

"Think I could stay with you tonight? Or would Dad just send Emmie?"

The monitor *beep beep beeps*.

Wren's equivalent for, *he'd send Emmie*. Or maybe she's wondering why I'm reading old House archives on my digislate instead of the story I promised we'd finish together.

"I know." I balance the slate on my knees. "But this one's on medichips."

If her old chip could have saved her, then a new one should wake her up.

Beep beep beep.

Medichips are a Westlet technology, and so far no one in our House has duplicated it. Dad got Wren's chip forever ago, from a potential House alliance that fell through. I'd fly to Westlet and ask for another, but Dad closed our borders so we can't communicate with other Houses in the Triplicate. Not Westlet or Galton. I've scanned Wren's palm to access the higher-level military networks, but out-of-House information just doesn't exist anymore. Dad disabled the communication satellites with the lockdown.

Wren says it used to be anybody who could access the House Triplicate newsfeeds. That people could log onto their digislates and read the gossip in Westlet. She says Mom used to gather her and me and Emmie on the big couch in our living room to watch feedshows from Galton.

I don't remember, wasn't old enough. Mom disappeared with the last of our uleum reserves and never looked back. If not for ecoflux, our whole House would have gone dark. No energy, no heat, no fuel.

Beepbeepbeep beep.

I refocus on my digislate. Plain text, no audio, and no new information on how to build a medichip. A muggy breeze rustles the curtains as Wren's monitor maintains a rhythm. I lay a palm to her chest. It rises and falls, normal and steady like always.

That's okay then.

I tap out of the database and load our latest book. "Let's see, where were we . . . *I don't know what made me look up, but when the battle smoke cleared, there he stood, the Death Ghost himself—"*

Beepbeepbeep beep beepbeepbeep beep.

"Wren?" I check the pulse in her neck. Regular, steady. Her color is good and the monitor's blue brainwave line weaves, rises, and—

Spikes into the "normal" zone.

Beep beepbeepbeep beep.

Another blue mountain crests the control line. Drifts across the screen.

The room shrinks or the monitor grows until there's only that towering spike amid a valley of hills. It reaches the screen's edge and disappears.

"Wren?" I'm on my knees, leaning close, one hand on her heart. "Wren, can you hear me?"

Her lashes don't flutter, but the mountain was *there.* More than one. I press the CALL button and yell for the floor medic. Aston barrels in, long white coat flapping.

"It spiked!" I point to the monitor. "The line, the blue one, it *spiked.*"

I SLAP MY PALM TO THE GLOWING SCANNER AND THE elevator kicks on automatically. Up forty-two floors to the very top of Axis Tower. Home. I bounce on my heels. The tower is made of offices and official House employees, but as soon as security registers me or my family, it shoots straight up to our suite.

If only it would move *faster*.

I tap my digislate on for the hundredth time. Aston loaded the monitor's readout with its beautiful, spiking mountains.

Wren is waking up.

Not yet, but she could be. She's improving. Dreaming a possibility she didn't even dare before, because it never spiked.

When the elevator reaches our suite, I sprint toward the living room and kick off my shoes in the mini entrance hall.

"Emmie! Dad!"

Sunset sings through the windowed wall, showcasing the city in starbursts and our living room in dust mites. I bound over Emmie's plushy armchair and through the arch into the study.

"No." Emmie's voice. Emmie's shout. *"No."*

I skid. Ahead lies the study, and the heavy white door to Dad's office.

"I am a Daughter of *Fane*. You can't sell me off!"

"Who do you think 'Fane' is?" Dad says in a tone normally reserved for me.

I set the digislate on the low table and creep across the furry rugs. Emmie has a thing about closed doors—even her bedroom's—so this one's open, too.

But not enough to see.

"What?" Emmie bites. "Am I supposed to reenact you and Mom all over again? So which of us sells the other out to Galton, me or him?"

"Emmaline."

I rock back, even though I'm unseen and barricaded.

Emmie probably doesn't flinch.

"The whole point of an alliance is for protection against Galton. With Westlet's backing, we might survive an invasion. Possibly," Dad says.

"You think Galton will invade?"

"If they learn of the Blight?" He sighs and I can almost hear him rubbing his head. "We're the perfect target. They'll gut us for uleum like the independents."

The independents are planets within the Triplicate but outside House borders—with no protection except their own single-planet militaries, which was how Galton was able to gut them.

Dad flew us to a strip-mined planet once, after all the

uleum had been extracted. A dried husk with a gaping wound we could see from space. Even after the Blight—even at the height of it—Urnath wasn't half as broken.

"But we're in lockdown!" Emmie says. "No communication in or out. They can't know. And besides, it's *over*. The factories work, the Blight's gone, so who cares if they know or not?"

"Urnath is *wasted*. Do you have any idea how much of our population that single planet fed? Over half, maybe three-quarters. I have finally built an open energy source for our people, only to turn around and instill rations on food. Not fuel, *food*."

"And you think Westlet's going to feed us in exchange for me?" Emmie is shrill, but Dad doesn't waver.

"Yes. They are."

A treaty. He means a marriage treaty with Westlet.

No. He can't. He absolutely can't. Emmie is *ours*.

My hand flattens on the door.

"Why can't Asa do it?" she asks. "Ship Wren off with her, and neither of them would even notice the difference."

I jerk back, fist my hand tight against my chest.

"She can't." Sighed and tired. Like he wishes I could.

"Why the hell not? She's—"

"Not firstborn," he finishes.

"Neither am I!"

"No. Not yet."

Wren. Birthrights transfer. If the oldest dies, the next oldest becomes Heir. It's the only way to become Heir.

"You're unplugging Wren," says Emmie, almost as flat as Dad.

"Westlet won't accept an alliance without the proxy power of an Heir. I don't have a choice."

No.

No, no. *"No."*

Three heavy steps and the door flies open. Dad fills the frame, nostrils flaring. He seems to sway with the tilting room.

Or maybe it's me.

"Asa."

"Mountains," I say with thick lips that won't move. "Dad, the mountains, you can't—"

"Can't what?" Emmie appears at his shoulder. "Sell me off? Or just unplug your precious Wren?"

"Emmaline," Dad says.

"Don't you mean *Lady Westlet*?"

His hand fists on the door.

"Please." I glance between them and lock onto Emmie— backlit and shiny in her stark white dress. "Wren's monitor spiked today, I have the readout, Aston—"

"Oh no," Emmie fires back. "You do not get to make this

about *her*. She won't be paraded down the aisle to a total stranger or—"

"Then I'll do it!" My words, my voice. My brain didn't even know.

But I don't take them back.

Emmie's eyebrows almost soar off her head. "What?"

I don't stop or think because this is Wren, so thinking doesn't matter. "I'll be the treaty. Leave Wren alone and I'll marry whoever you want."

His eyes flash and Emmie's mouth opens, but the silence stays.

"It doesn't work like that," Dad says.

Careful. I have to be careful and calm. I know a lot about alliances after researching medichips. There are different kinds and different levels, but none *require* an Heir.

"A bond treaty just needs a Son or Daughter. Any Son or Daughter. It doesn't have to be Emmie."

"Asa."

"I'll be a good wife. I won't complain or argue or anything."

Dad's jaw tightens, his lips press thin.

"Unless I'm supposed to, then I will. I'll argue all the time."

His hand slides off the door to rub the graying roots of his hair. "You are not a power, Asa. Westlet cannot rule this

House through you. He's offering his Heir and wants mine. No Heir, no alliance."

Emmie balls her hands. "And that will be the end of the universe, will it?"

"Yes," says Dad. "We'll starve."

"WE ARE *NOT* STARVING," I SAY. "DAD DOESN'T KNOW what he's talking about. I went and bought icelees for the medics today. And puffcakes. And three sticky rolls this morning. And I know what starving looks like and this is not *it*."

Emmie sits cross-legged on her big four-poster bed, back to the wall, arms pulled close over her dress. A pale knot amid black blankets and pillows. "He's going to do it. He's really going to do it."

"If the Blight had hit everywhere and everyone was starving, then maybe—but it didn't and they're *not*." I slap both hands on the window, press my nose to the pane. The night glimmers haze, deep purples and blues. Skytowers sing toward the horizon, multilevel monoliths threaded with tiny white windows. And through one of them, Wren dreams of mountains and monitors and one day waking up.

"Not again. Not again, not again."

I'm not killing her again.

"They won't let me meet him. I don't even get to *see* him," Emmie runs both hands back and forth over her head, until her hair frizzes a halo.

"What?"

She grabs the digislate by her feet and tosses it to the end of the bed. "Some stupid Westlet thing. This traditional 'blood bond' ceremony that's supposed to make it all irrevocable."

43

I spin, shoot across the room to clamber on the bed. "They want to cut you *open*?"

"No." Emmie pushes me away hard enough I fall on my elbows, and scoots back along the bed. "God, Asa, how do you even dream this stuff up?"

"You said blood, I just thought—what's it mean then?"

"It *means* I can't get out. Ever. It 'fuses' our bloodlines to make the treaty unbreakable. No divorce, no separation, even if he dies I'm still married to his damn ghost."

I sit up. "But they can't—"

"Yes, they can." She jerks her head at the tossed digi-slate. "Look."

The slate is off somehow, odd. Different, thinner, its standby screen dim and gray. No color. I tap the screen, but nothing happens.

"You have to use the buttons," Emmie says. "It's one of *theirs*."

"From Westlet?" I twist the slate toward the light and there they are. Buttons. Marked with circles and arrows and running down both sides. I hit three before the screen changes. Black text on a flat background, long words and formal phrases with no give, no recourse. No out.

"Dad's *signing* this?"

Emmie's grin could kill. "Did you see my dress?"

"Your dress?"

She crawls over and reaches across me, pressing buttons until the screen scrolls to the end. "Isn't it pretty? I hear suffocation is in this year."

The dress covers every inch of skin—eyes, mouth, hands—as if anyone could even walk under all that.

"Well?" asks Emmie. "What do you think?"

I trace the anonymous fabric outline. "Make you a deal."

Emmie rolls her eyes and asks the ceiling, "What?"

"Keep Dad from killing Wren."

She falls backward, bounces on the pillows. "Of course, of *course*."

"Please, just until after the wedding. Tell him—tell him you can't walk down the aisle with her dead."

Emmie rises, snatches the slate from my hand to thrust it in my face. "*Look*. This will be *me*. Can't you focus for five damn seconds on anything not *her*?" She throws the digislate at the bed's edge, and it skitters off the coverlet to the floor. "What if he's a bastard? What if they've only pulled out this whole blood bond thing because no one would have him otherwise? What if he's *vicious*, Asa? What if he's like *Mom*?"

No, Dad wouldn't marry us to someone vicious. Not vicious. He wouldn't, not even to save our House.

I don't think he would.

"Please, Emmie. I'll make it worth it. I'll stick close

and do whatever you need before the wedding, and when it's time to get ready I'll lock everyone out and help you get dressed."

"Oh!" Her fingers flutter in the moonlight, silver rings and shiny nails. "You'll dress me! I can hardly wait!"

I glance at the slightly open door, lower my voice. "I'll give you Mom's sparkle bracelet."

Emmie's hand stops, midflight.

Dad boxed up everything of Mom's after she left. Wren said he shipped it to her in Galton, Emmie thinks he destroyed it. Either way, Emmie has nothing of hers and neither do I.

The bracelet is Wren's.

"I thought she threw it away," Emmie says.

I shrug. "She told Dad so."

She'd just taken on some of her bigger responsibilities as Heir and thought it'd make him happy.

Emmie sucks on her lip. "Where is it?"

Wren's closet, lowest shelf, inside her favorite fuzzy socks.

My feet get cold sometimes.

"The deal first. You'll protect Wren?" I hold out my hand.

Emmie sighs, but takes it anyway. "Fine, deal. Now, where's the bracelet?"

BONDS

EMMIE SITS BEFORE THE MIRROR AND TRIES TO make up for all the sleep she didn't get. Layer after layer of cream and eye shadow, the white dresser strewn with half-empty tubes. She's in her sleep bra and pants so that nothing gets on the airy lace dress she brought from home—made special to fit under the ceremonial dress. Her clothes cases take up the entire corner of the guest bedroom. We flew into the Westlet House complex late last night.

Emmie leans into her reflection, draws a tight black line along her lid. "Is the dress ready?"

My throat's so dry it cracks. "On the door."

"No, the other one."

"On the bed." The heavy Westlet overdress swallows the mattress, draped sleeves hanging off the sides. A brown satin cone with white lace overlays to match the opaque headdress propped on the pillow.

Emmie straightens before the silver winged mirror. Bare shoulders pulled back, red lips stark above her lifted chin. Elegance and sovereignty despite the still frizzed mess of hair. "Get my curler, would you?"

I nod. Scramble to open the clothes case near the bed. Grab the worn gray handle of her favorite hair curler. Then my toe catches on the bed's edge and it clatters to the floor.

Emmie jumps. "God, Asa! Can't you keep hold of anything? Just this *once*?"

I retrieve the curler. "I'm sorry, I'm—"

"Do I need to get one of those Westlet people in here? Have *them* dress me?"

"No! I've got it, I swear—"

"Then *prove* it."

I blink hard, harder, and can't stop.

Then Emmie's blinking, too. "You can't cry. You promised Dad you wouldn't cry."

"I'm not." And maybe the words are watery, but my cheeks aren't. They can't be, not yet.

"Yes, you are." Emmie sinks into the dresser, elbows buried in lip gloss and compacts. I can't see her eyes in the mirror.

Which means she can't see me.

Now. It has to be now.

I set the curler on the bed and inch closer. "You don't have to worry."

"This isn't one of your stories, Asa. Words don't make things real."

"They can if you back them up."

"God, you and Wren." She snorts, then shakes her head. "Do me a favor?"

"Anything." Another step.

"Don't spend your life in the medicenter. Travel or study or find some love-struck idiot and have a bus-full of babies. Just *do* something. One of us should."

"It's okay, promise." I brush the cascade of hair away from the side of her neck. Wait for her to flinch.

She doesn't. Her shoulders shake with the harsh rhythm of her breath. "Sure it is."

She's not crying. We don't cry.

And when we do, we fix it.

I reach into my pocket. "I love you. Don't forget."

She chokes, half laughs. "I'm not Wren, in case you haven't noticed."

"Of course not, you're you," I say and press the injector pen against her neck.

EVEN WITHOUT SHOES, I'M TALLER THAN EMMIE. DAD hasn't noticed, though his steps clack with his shiny ceremony boots and mine don't. We walk and walk and still the marble hall stretches forever—its intense white walls arching at least three stories high. Painted. Not with colorbot paint, no shimmery circuits, but with something rich and dead.

Ahead the white floors and walls converge on two massive orange doors, silver-edged and flanked by men in silver uniforms. A special kind of silver caught between ice and snow. House colors. Westlet colors.

It's just us and them and the brush of my dress on the marble. The heavy sleeves swallow my fingers, which is good because they shake. A lot. I barely got it on, and had to ask the woman stationed outside the dressing room to do up the clips in back. I put on my best Emmie voice and told her my sister was sleeping and should be left alone. The orderly's face was fuzzy through my veil, but she nodded and didn't try to come in.

"Keep your head up," whispers Dad. "Don't slouch."

I straighten. Hot, thick air burns my nose and sticks in my throat.

One step, three.

We stop.

The men bow. To me first, then to Dad next and more

deeply, and then they pull open the doors. Sunlight floods the floor, Dad and me. Somewhere beyond, a woman sings. A delicate and almost touchable song of crystalized winters where the frost doesn't burn.

Emmie's favorite lullaby. The one Wren would hum because she couldn't remember the words.

I stop dead.

"You said it was your favorite," Dad says.

It was. Is. Both Emmie's and Wren's. The notes have claws, digging deep and dragging out all the things I can't think about like travel and study and love-struck—

"Emmaline?" Dad asks.

What if he's vicious? What if he's like Mom?

"Emmaline."

No, he's not, he won't be. If Emmie had to marry him, I can, too. I will step forward. Right now. This second.

I *will*.

My knee bends, my foot lifts, and I'm through the doors.

Dad squeezes my arm. Acknowledgment, not directive.

Flower petals trail over a sunbaked stone veranda and catch along my socks as I navigate the wide, shallow steps. The people lining the pathway are all in Westlet uniforms, straight-backed orderlies in staring silver rows. And past them, at the very end, he waits. The House Heir. Lord Eagle is dressed in as many layers as I am, though his overdress has a helmet instead of a veil. Probably easier to breathe through.

We won't see each other until after the ceremony, when we're no longer the walking embodiment of the Fane and Westlet bloodlines, but simply Asa and Eagle.

Not Eagle and Emmie.

Walk, just walk.

Dad grips my arm, and we follow the petals until they stop.

Eagle's taller than me.

Or it could be the helmet—orange-lined steel with thread-thin eye slits.

We bow. To the white-robed Officiator, to my dad and Eagle's parents stationed off to the left, to each other. Lady Westlet beams sunshine while the Lord scans us with bored, languid eyes.

Dad has no expression at all.

The Officiator steps forward. I face the boy in the helmet and hold out my hands. We can't show any skin during the ceremony, but we can't have any fabric between our palms, either. One's against the rules, and the other's bad luck. I bunch the bottom edge of my sleeve just inside the cuff like I helped Emmie practice, so Eagle can reach in.

My hands shake, but not enough to notice.

Except Eagle does.

His left hand finds mine—his rough and mine hot—but his right fumbles. Twists through the fabric in all the wrong ways and I can't feel his skin. Seconds slip into clusters. My sleeve has a mind of its own, dancing with my trembling arm and his unsteady fingers. A swear floats from behind the helmet. Everyone watches and pretends not to.

We're telling a story and it's the wrong one.

Marriage should be happy. Nobody shakes.

I focus on the stone under my feet. Solid and impenetrable like I need to be. Like I *am*. A rock. A skytower.

A Daughter of Fane.

My fingers still and his finally lock on, skin to skin.

I sag, but it doesn't matter because the Officiator opens the ceremony.

That's it, the worst of it. Now we just stand until the bell sounds. Then we'll be married, and after that it won't matter.

My knuckles are lost under Eagle's wide palms. He squeezes my right hand tight, like he needs the leverage, but he grips my left with loose, oddly waxy fingers.

Rather like Casser's. He'd lost a hand when he was a kid and had a biotech replacement—one that merged digital parts with living cells. When it glitched, he had trouble gripping, too.

I feel along Eagle's wrist for the telltale seam between

fake skin and real. It's there, light as a scratch after the scab's gone, easy to miss. Maybe Westlet had ration riots, too. Maybe he got caught in one.

Eagle goes still. Shoulders set, hands rigid. I twist my hands up and squeeze both of his.

He's *awake*. Alive and standing. If Wren could be all those things or even half, she'd give up her hand in a heartbeat.

"And thus are you united," the Officiator breaks from monotone. "By bond and by blood."

The bell rings, a kick deep in my stomach. I flinch and so does Eagle, but the tolling continues. Once for Westlet, once for Fane, and once for both together. A deep, echoing toll that can't be taken back.

Married. We're married.

The white cuffs of Dad's suit shine bright against his brown sleeves. He stands straight and strong as ever, but lighter somehow, head tipped back to the cloudless sky.

My heart tolls with the bell.

Eagle lets go and my heavy sleeve drags down my arm. We face the hushed gathering. Some smile, but most don't. Not even when a cheer goes up.

Eagle holds out his arm, and we walk down the aisle under a rainstorm of petals.

ALONE. WE'RE ALONE. IN A ROOM OVERTAKEN BY A saccharine floral army. Flowers are everywhere, bell-shaped blue and yellow, vased and hanging.

In Westlet blood bond tradition, we get to see each other before we present ourselves to our parents.

Eagle moves between the flowers with purpose, pulling at the string near his throat. His overdress slides to the floor, revealing a silver suit with burnt-orange cuffs. He reaches for his helmet.

Westlet didn't send us any pictures of Eagle, but Dad may have offered pictures of Emmie.

"Wait," I say, so fast I squeak. If he knows first, maybe he won't be as mad. With his helmet on, I won't have to know how mad he is.

The slitted metal eyes swing my way, but only for a moment. "They're expecting us."

"Not yet." I step forward, hand out and up. "Just wait."

"You'll have to see me sometime." His voice is odd, scratchy, biting off each word.

"Please?" I try again. *"Please."*

He stands, a fabric statue with eyes I can't see.

"Please *what*?" He steps closer. "Never take it off?"

He hates me. He will hate me even more.

My tongue knots with my fingers and my sleeves and the tangles in my head.

Say it, just *say* it.

He shakes his head and steps away, hands rising.

"I'm not Emmie!"

His fingers freeze at his helmet's edge. The medics misjudged his skin tone, so his waxy right hand is pale brown instead of the near black of his real one.

A stark, impenetrable, "What?"

"I'm Asa. Not Emmie. Emmaline."

"Asa."

"The youngest, you know—well, maybe not, with the lockdown—unless you saw me before that? Except I wasn't very old then and I don't know how old you were or if you remember, though you probably wouldn't because it wasn't your House so why would it matter, but I *am* Fane. Still blood. We are still bonded and allied and everything."

"You're not the Heir," he says.

"No, but I am Fane and that's all that matters—"

"Your father planned this?"

"No! I did! I mean, it was my idea. Dad doesn't know. You think he would have played that song otherwise? During the ceremony? The lullaby? That's Emmie's favorite, not mine. Ask anyone. If he knew, he'd have played 'Frostlark' or . . . or something."

God, all you do is babble, I can hear Emmie say.

The meshy veil is thick and hot and sticking to my lips.

I tug at the headdress, bend down to pull it over my head, but it doesn't budge—it's clipped tight in too many places I can't reach. I yank again and knock into a little table by the chair. I hear a vase crash, feel water splashing my feet and flowers crumpling.

I hug my sleeved palms to my chest so I can't break anything else.

A hard exhale. "Hold on."

Eagle sidesteps the mess and circles behind me. A muffled *thump*, and then his helmet rolls past my feet to bounce against a chair. Fingers skim my shoulders, find the clips, undo the buttons. I let my arms fall as he grasps the sides of the headdress. "Ready?"

"Yeah." I stretch my neck to make it easy. Brace for the yank that'll tug out what little hair I have. The veil feels cemented to my head.

Except Eagle is careful. Avoids my ears. A couple strands catch, then the world expands unfiltered—cool air filling my overhot lungs. I look over my shoulder. "Thank . . ."

The right half of his face, cheek to ear and neck to temple, has been burned. Skin puckered, folded and shiny. Ridged in places, grated in others. Shallow, unsteady rivers weave around his right eye, twist the corner of his mouth. The left side is smooth, mostly untouched, like someone took a ruler and drew half a map.

"Still thrilled with your idea?" he says, and his large brown eyes say nothing and everything at once.

"Yes."

A long incredulous second, then he dumps the head-dress with a *thud*. Unfastens the buttons down my back and pushes the overdress off my shoulders. I shake my arms from the sleeves and kick out of the crumpled fabric.

My underdress is simple, wide-necked and knee-length, pale brown trimmed in white. House colors. Fane colors.

Eagle stares. At me, my legs. Or rather, my feet. At least I remembered socks, so he can't see my nail-less toes. Aston promises they'll regrow, like he promises my hair will someday be long enough to run my fingers through instead of over.

"Shoes?" he asks, like he's counting straws and this one is second to last.

I shake my head. "I'm taller than Emmie."

MY FEET DON'T MATTER, MY FACE IS ENOUGH. DAD fades as white as the couch he sits on, then glows red as the wine in his hand. "Asa?"

"Asa?" asks someone. Eagle's parents? Followed by, "Eagle?"

"She's the youngest," says the boy who was at my side and isn't anymore.

I'm alone.

Dad becomes everything deliberate and careful. Sets his wine glass on the table without a clink and stands without a sound. Chiseled edges and conversational tone. "Where is Emmaline?"

"Sedated." I push past the weight of my tongue. "Sleeping. She's okay."

"Sedated."

"You were going to kill her."

"Fane?" asks that someone again, but it doesn't matter. My father steps forward.

I back away. "It's all right, I swear it's all right. I'm blood so the alliance still holds—"

"Shut. Up." Dad blocks the light, and my heels hit the wall. "Tell me I didn't walk *you* down that aisle." His chest heaves as his hands flex. "Tell me."

"She's going to wake up." My voice is tinny even in my head. "Her monitor—"

"*Tell me!*" Dad's fist sails past my ear and slams the wall near my head. I press flat, but there's nowhere to run.

"*Fane!*" A larger, darker hand latches onto Dad's arm and yanks him back. "I don't know what game you're playing, but you will *not* play it here."

Lord Westlet is taller than Dad, leaner and wider cheeked. Fluid water, but every bit as frigid.

"Please," I say. "It was me. Dad didn't know. I drugged Emmie—"

"Shut up, Asa," Dad growls, and Lord Westlet chimes in with, "Yes, child, *do.*"

Neither looks at me. The air crackles.

"You know, Fane," Lord Westlet continues, "it is one thing to undercut the one, the only stipulation I had in this agreement when *you* were the one to approach us, but *this*?"

"We can solve this, I will do whatever—"

"You think there is a *solution*?"

"—is necessary, whatever is necessary."

"Please," I say, louder now, "it wasn't him, I—"

"*You?*" Lord Westlet rounds on me, then drops Dad's arm in disgust. His lips catch between a smile and a scream as he turns to his wife. "I knew this was a trick. The glorious Fane appearing from the mists after thirteen years—*thirteen*—of no contact whatsoever. Though even *I* wouldn't have thought him capable of making his child—"

"He was going to kill Wren!" I yell loud enough the stars hear me.

Silence. A thousand tugging strings from four sets of eyes.

"Emmie's not the Heir," I rush out before somebody stops me, "not unless Wren dies, and Wren isn't dead. Dad was going to pull her life support to make Emmie what you wanted. But I won't be Heir even if Wren dies, so she's safe now. I'll be a good wife, I swear, and Emmie will take care of Wren."

Dad stands straight and unmoving and somehow leveled to the bone.

"Wren?" asks Lord Westlet. "Your oldest? But you said—"

"She's in a coma," Dad says. "Over six months now. Her chances are minimal, and the last specialist recommended life support removal three months ago."

"You mean Marianne?" I ask. "No, Dad, you can't listen to her. She wants to pull everybody! The whole ward talks about it, just ask—"

Dad's hand cuts the air with a silent, *stop*, and my words die.

In sync and on cue, the older Westlets glance at their son.

Eagle looks like he's been in a hundred hospitals with

63

a hundred specialists who measure out cheery platitudes that never add up to hope. But he's still here, tall like his dad with his mother's poise, dressed in their colors and part of their conversation without having to say a word.

"I have a daughter who will never wake," Dad says, slow and coarse. "An ally who would only become an ally in exchange for my Heir. I have a new, sustainable fuel my people don't trust, because its creation cost us our main agricultural planet. I've had to release half my troops because I cannot afford their rations. The one thing standing between me and a Galton invasion is a lockdown that was never intended to last half this long, and likely won't last much longer. Do you think I'd be here if I had a choice? Any other choice?"

The silence vibrates, hinges on Dad's rigid frame. "Do you think I would be here if I had any other out? Do you want me on my knees? Because I will beg."

No. He wouldn't, he *can't*.

The room tastes of rust and acid, and I can't look away.

He's lying, he has to be. He's our *House*. He stands for everybody. Fane doesn't beg, *Fane* would never—

Dad steps forward, right knee folding down.

"No!" I clutch his arm. "Don't! You *can't*. It's my fault, I'll fix it, I promise, Dad, I swear."

He doesn't look at me. "Let go, Asa."

Lord Westlet looks between us. "This is . . ." He presses two long fingers between his eyes. "No. Enough. Get out."

"Westlet," says Dad in a voice that could almost be mine.

The Lord rounds on him and points to the door I entered by. "To the other room, Fane, for five minutes—five damn minutes. I need to speak with my family."

Dad doesn't move. "The treaty stands?"

Lord Westlet throws up his arms. "It's inviolate, that was the whole point of a blood bond! Of course it stands."

"And the food shipments?"

The Lord's teeth glitter. "One thing at a time."

DAD DOESN'T YELL. HIS STEPS OWN EVERY LAST INCH of the room as I curl in a chair, but he doesn't yell. He doesn't have to.

I am a stupid reckless child. A disappointment. The shame of our House, *my* House, whom I've just doomed to starve.

I am my mother's daughter.

Mom orchestrated the theft of our last, unpopulated uleum-rich planet. Used her power as Lady of Fane to sneak Galton soldiers in. Seized the mine that was supposed to see our House through the development of ecoflux and make the transition easy instead of a ration nightmare. She tried to break our House, but we survived her.

We may not survive me.

"Enough, Dad." Emmie stands in the doorway, barefoot in sleep pants and a silver-orange robe that doesn't suit her and doesn't belong. "It's done."

He halts and transfers all his flame to her.

One shot of this and you'll be down for the night, Aston had said when I went to the medic's desk for something to help me sleep. He hadn't even questioned it.

But Emmie's eyes are red and her skin is pasty, like someone drugged her.

Me.

"You don't know what she's done," Dad says. "The *extent*

of it. You have no idea."

Emmie shrugs. "I know she can't take it back, and that if you keep this up she'll be a blubbering mess on the floor and *that* won't go over well. You know how she is."

"Yes."

A disgrace. Unfit for my colors, unfit for my name.

"We're ready for you." Lord Westlet slides in, eyes only for Dad. "And just you. The children stay out."

EMMIE GIVES ME SHOES. HER SHOES, AND A HOODED cape deep enough to hide my face. She marches through rooms and corridors, pale heels pounding paler wood until wood turns to stone, and rooms to air.

When she stops, I stop, too.

"Try not to be an ass. There's been enough of that today."

"I'm sorry," I say.

Emmie swears and grabs my shoulders. "How did you think this would go down? Huh? What did you think Dad would say? How could you possibly be so *stupid*?"

"I don't know."

"Not. Good. Enough." She shakes me until my head wobbles. "What do you think will happen to Wren now? Dad will probably unplug her out of spite."

"No, he won't." I look up, her face inches away. "You'll look after her. When you're not traveling and studying and all that."

Her lips thin, and her nails dig into my skin, her shiny eyes catching the sun before she squeezes them tight. She shakes her head, flips me around, and pushes. I stumble forward into longer arms and a different, harder chest.

"Damn stupid idiot," she mutters, then adds louder, "earn yourself some cosmic favors and *don't* be an ass."

"Okay," I say to Emmie's retreating steps.

"She meant me," says Eagle.

EAGLE'S BOOTS MAKE LESS SOUND THAN EMMIE'S heels. I keep my head down, away from the flowered trees. Focus on the stone puzzle pattern of the walkway. It doesn't matter where we are or where we're going. Dad will find me soon enough.

The path ends in a small tower less than ten stories tall, with silver walls broken by an arched door and high round windows. Eagle doesn't enter a code or palm a security screen, he just pulls the door open.

We step into a tiny, private docking bay, with overhead lights powered down to almost nothing. A flightwing commands most of the space, its curved wingtip nearly brushing Eagle's head. He leads me to a small elevator, which rises so fast my stomach drops. The doors open, Eagle snaps his fingers, and light flares.

I lift my head and the hood slides off.

A long, wide room. White walls with no pictures, two white chairs and a couch with no pillows, pale floorboards with no scuffs. Even the stone balcony, peeking through the glass doors in the wall opposite, is white.

Stark and empty.

Eagle is as silent as the room, but Dad echoes in my head.

I hadn't left home since Decontamination. I'd stayed in the capital city on our core planet, within a three-district radius of Wren's medicenter and Axis Tower. Of course no one was starving. Of our whole House, Malsa would have been the last place to fall.

I rub my shoulders. "He will send the food, won't he? Your dad? He'll send the food?"

"A blood bond's inviolate." Which should be an affirmation, except his voice says if it wasn't, the bond would be ripped to shreds.

The floor sucks me in.

"Easy." Eagle grabs my arms as my knees give out, holds on until I find my feet.

But Fane doesn't break, not in front of people.

I step into the barren white room and Eagle lets go. Ahead, two doors glare at each other across the floor, each ajar. Bedrooms? Maybe? Something else?

My arms won't warm no matter how much I rub them. I try twice before words come out. "Do we share?"

"You're in that one." Eagle jerks his chin at the door on the left, then disappears through the one on the right.

RINGING. IN MY EARS, MY BONES. A STEADY WHINE THAT rises and fills everything. Is everything. It crushes. Flattens me between hard pavement and limp heat. Smoke in my nose, dust and iron. It's on my cheeks, sliding through my hair and down my neck. "Wren?" Heat puddles in my ringing ear, slithers through my parted lips. I taste blood. "Wren?"

I jerk awake. Scramble back until my shoulders hit a wall. Rub my face and ear and neck, because they're all sticky and seeping and Wren—

Wren.

I fumble to my knees, fight the ringing echoes. Search the ground. She's here, I know she's here, I can still feel her on my chest and—

The floor bounces, fuzzy with blankets. A bed, not an alley. A dark room with a desk in the corner and two doors in the walls. No rising smoke, no bleeding Wren.

Just me.

"It's okay," I say aloud because that usually helps.

But it doesn't. I reach for my digislate with its library of audiostories to erase the one in my head, except it's not here. I can't find it in the covers. I don't know where it's gone, or if it's even here.

I curl forward, ears burning with blood that isn't there. The room squeezes tight and I have to get out. Somewhere, anywhere. See what the stars look like from a different solar system. See if I can see home.

The living room is dim; Eagle's door is closed tight. I creep past the couch and end table to the balcony's sliding glass doors and slip through. Find the night and the stars.

And Eagle. Eagle's on the balcony. Leaning against the fenced edge, forearms loose on the curved railing.

He doesn't speak, doesn't smile. Probably hates me. I know Dad does.

I mean, his dad, not mine. Probably not mine.

Eagle looks away. His suit's smooth lines are unbroken by wrinkles. It's the same one from yesterday.

I step forward and the words are out before my brain catches up. "Make you a deal."

He doesn't turn. "Shoot."

"I don't want . . ." But the words sound stupid in my head and they'll be worse on my tongue, and I can't not say them because I've already started and why did I come out here at all?

"Me to touch you? Got it," he says a half second before I get out, "Us to hate each other."

Shadows shift and I *feel* it. The full weight of his attention.

"No, I mean Emmie said it wasn't—that the agreement said we could wait until, that it wasn't expected yet."

A lower, less icy, "What?"

My face burns. "Not that we won't know each other at

some point, but we don't now, if you don't mind, if we could just wait—"

"No."

Oh.

I hug Emmie's cloak, soak in what's left of her scent. Gingernut and confidence. She's good with boys. I've gone out some, mostly with Jordi before the Blight, but it didn't last that long or go that far but the kissing was nice. Not scary.

Not like this.

Eagle swears half under his breath, then says, "Yes."

"What?"

"Earlier." Slow and careful. "Before. What don't you want?"

I tug my sleeves over my fingertips, twist the ends. Emmie's coat, Emmie's place. She'd know what to say.

She wouldn't have said anything to begin with.

"Us to hate each other forever." I raise my head. "That's a really long time."

The night soaks up his expression and I slide a step back. "Never mind, I'll just—"

"Deal," he says.

I freeze. "What?"

He pushes off the rail and walks straight toward me. I lock my legs so they don't back up. But he doesn't try to tower, or even slow down as he passes by.

"You should get ready. They'll want us in an hour."

REPRISAL

"YOU ARE DESPERATELY IN LOVE," SAYS LADY Westlet, her hair a wide cape brushing her sleek shoulders. She radiates blue and silver, a skirt billowing over long legs that float across the floor. She could be Emmie's age or mine, crisp and sparkling in the pink sunrise through the curtainless windows.

The summons came in an hour exactly. Eagle is clairvoyant.

Dad stands near the end table, wide-legged and with one hand behind his back. Lord Westlet leans against a yellow cabinet and examines his nails. Neither speaks as the Lady points a long graceful finger at the son who could be her mirror image, despite the scars. Eagle's fresh suit matches her perfect dress and the meticulous room with its symmetrical bamboo rugs. Eagle leans into the couch's white cushions while I sit on its very edge, smoothing my wrinkled skirt.

I had nothing to change into.

"You've been corresponding secretly for months." Lady Westlet swishes past, sketching the outlines of our past in the air. "Terrified of the consequences. Breaking your father's lockdown. Consorting with the daughter of the enemy."

They consider Fane an enemy?

She bends over us with wide red lips. Eagle isn't human; he doesn't retreat.

"Love letters." Mint and petals. "Last year, while Eagle rebuilt his strength in the medicenter, you two wrote almost constantly."

"Wrote?" I ask. "I wouldn't have wrote."

Her lips thin as Eagle straightens, and spiders dance under my skin.

"I'd have been there, at the medicenter. You can't just write. What if the medics kept him drugged or messed up his meds or—"

"Enough." Lady Westlet taps my nose. Steps back until the window washes sunlight through her hair. "Then came the perfect chance. You," she says, waving at me, "drugged your sister and stole her marriage robes, while you," she continues while smiling at Eagle, "waited happily for your bride. No inherent betrayal or treachery, only two children in love."

"And you think they'll buy it?" Dad asks with careful neutrality.

From his corner, Lord Westlet flicks invisible dust from

his sleeve. "Let us hope so, Fane, for your sake."

"People will always 'buy' love," says the Lady. "Especially of the forbidden variety. The feeds do love a good scandal. Besides, why else would our dear Fane jeopardize an alliance he claims so desperately to need?"

"But he didn't," I say. "It was—"

"You?" Lord Westlet pushes off the cabinet and crosses to the ornate mirror on the far wall. Adjusts his collar. His face is reflected large against the backdrop of us. "The Heir was an asset. You are not. Therefore, we must convince the Electorate that you *are*."

"The Elec—?"

His eyes meet mine in the mirror. "Fane stands with us in all things. You are our proof. You will do what we tell you, when we tell you, and love whom we say. You will show yourself faithful and keep the Electorate happy, otherwise all food shipments are forfeit. Is that clear?"

They all turn to me. Lady Westlet's arched brows. Eagle's scarred rivers of expressionless ice. Dad's disowning eyes and mouthed *yes*.

My yes, is as silent as his. I swallow and repeat, "Yes."

"No, my lady." Lord Westlet moves from the mantel. He places a cool finger under my chin and lifts my face. "Your father has no power here. This bargain is between you and me."

My fault, my amends.

"I am faithful. I will be."

He brushes a stray tear away with a smooth, wide thumb. "None of that," he says. "I am not heartless. Your father won't leave empty-handed. Let's see, shall we say a third of the first promised shipment?"

"Westlet," Dad drags out the name, clips it off. A war between restraint and desperation. "I cannot supplement even base supplies with that."

The Lord's eyes never leave mine. "You can for a few months, after which you'll receive the second third—should our new dear daughter prove faithful." He traces my cheek with gentle fingers. "And you will prove faithful, dear, will you not?"

I straighten. "You have my word."

Lord Westlet's smile drifts between crystal and silk. "And rest assured, I'll hold you to it."

"YOU CAN'T TALK ABOUT URNATH." EMMIE DOUSES MY head in gel. I sit on my hands on the bed that's now mine, while she stands by my knees and feathers my hair. I need to be pretty for the press conference and Emmie volunteered. "Or Decontamination. Or how bad fuel rations were, or how our uleum ran out, or ecoflux, or the food shortage or—"

"They want to know how much I love Eagle," I say, "not what a ration token looks like."

She pulls back. "Not just the reporters, *anyone* outside the Westlets. Galton can't know."

"She wouldn't. How could she? Lady Galton isn't here."

Emmie yanks at the strands behind my ear and I squeak. "Because there's no lockdown here! Everything you say could get back to her. Did you even *read* the blood bond agreement before you hijacked it? Lockdown doesn't end until our House is stable enough to fend Galton off. Dad says not all the Electorate are loyal to Westlet. If you run your mouth, Galton will hear."

I twist away so she doesn't uproot my whole head. "What do you mean, the Elect—?"

"All it takes is one, Asa. One person, one word, one leak, and our lockdown is busted. Galton will know exactly how easy we'd be to invade. Then you'll have the satisfaction of knowing you not only starved us out but had our planets gutted, too."

I am holes with no structure, and still the weight presses in. Her eyes widen like she doesn't know where her anger came from or how to take it back.

Taking it back won't make it any less true.

Without the promised shipments, Dad will instate full rationing like Wren had to. Which will be okay for a while, until it isn't.

I've put my whole House in quarantine, with no Decontamination to get us out. Wren would kill me.

Better me than her.

Emmie rubs her forehead and sighs. "Look, Dad's staying off your back. But you have to promise me that you will not get chatty with people. No stories. No random conversations. No nonrandom conversations. In fact, just don't talk."

"If you're done," says a voice that isn't Emmie's. "We're needed."

We both jump and Emmie spins. Eagle fills the doorway.

"Don't you knock?" Emmie asks.

"It was open." He deliberately steps into the room and opens the door wider. Gives her room to pass.

Emmie straightens. Eagle either doesn't notice or doesn't care.

"Don't." I reach out, brush her arm, and her glare transfers to me. I brace for the volley. The next truth.

"Fine." She shakes me off and walks to the door, passing Eagle like he doesn't exist.

"Emmie—"

"I'll check on Wren." She disappears, and the *don't forget* dies on my tongue.

Eagle waits until the elevator pings. "You ready?"

I nod.

He steps into the room and the light from the window catches his face. Makeup, cream, foundation.

Wren's specialist tried that once, at the medicenter. Brought a wig to hide her skull.

"No." I'm on my feet, head shaking. "No, they can't, no."

I cross the room and this time Eagle backs up. "What?"

"This." I wave at his face, slathered as mine feels. "Makeup? You should have said no."

"You didn't."

"Yes, but I'm *faithful*."

"You think you're the only one?"

I try to make the words fit in my head. "But you're the Heir. You don't have to *be* anything."

He only moves to the door. "They're waiting."

"It won't take long." I grab his sleeve and tug him toward my spot on the bed. Push him down. "Stay." Then I run into the small bathroom off my bedroom and dig around in the cabinets. All the brands are odd, but cream remover

81

looks the same everywhere and there are washcloths in the drawers.

"What are you doing?" Eagle calls.

"Fixing it." I come back in, arms full.

"No," says Eagle.

"Yes." I cross the room and dump the lot beside him on the bed.

He is on his feet, a whole world taller than me. *"No."*

"*Yes*. You survived! You get to eat breakfast with your family every day and dinner with them every night. When people look at you, they should see courage—literally—in your skin, and face the idea that you didn't give up when they probably would have. You're *awake* and standing and if they don't realize how amazing that is, then you can just blame me."

His eyes are huge and mine wet and all that mascara Emmie spent so much time putting on is probably dripping everywhere. But everything's wrong enough already. This won't be, too. I cross my arms and lift my chin.

And Eagle sits down. Just like that.

I'M NOT PRETTY ENOUGH FOR LADY WESTLET. SHE looks us up and down and tells Eagle, "I could have sworn they said you were ready."

"They did," says Eagle.

"And this is ready?" she asks.

I open my mouth, but Eagle says, "Yes."

He crosses the airy room to the wide paneled window and gently parts the curtains. I don't know where we are exactly, but silver arches crisscross the high ceiling and elegant bluegrain chairs circle the inlaid tile floor. It's the kind of room to impress guests, with windows that likely open to the main veranda. Where the newsfeed reporters are.

"This is nowhere near ready." Lady Westlet rubs long fingers over my gelled head, flicks the tufted strands behind my ear. "Is this the latest fashion? In Fane?"

Actually, it is in places. Some people who weren't Decontaminated shaved their head in protest. Or maybe solidarity. Except their hair always grows back thick and full. Ours doesn't.

Which the Lady must already know, because Dad had to have told them about the Blight.

"Pity." The Lady sighs and lets go. "Your sister has such an excellent sense of style. Never mind. We'll just have to . . ." She grasps my shoulders and spins me around, grinning like a kid. "Oh, I am brilliant."

She skips away, if elegance is capable of skipping, and retrieves something from a glass bubble case along the far wall. "Turn around."

I do. So does Eagle, watching from the window. The Lady wraps a scarf around my head, then pins something to it by my right ear. A metal flower or light medallion. "Tight enough?"

I shake my head, test the hold. Nothing moves. "I think so."

"Excellent." She pulls me across the tile to deposit me in front of Eagle. "Voilà! What do you think?"

Nothing, or everything. His tight face says both.

"Never mind." Lady Westlet fluffs the ends of the scarf. "Your father-in-law will love it."

LADY WESTLET SELLS US. SHE STANDS ON THE VERANDA between the potted bellflowers, dress swishing orange and silver. Eagle and I sit to the left of her empty seat while Lord Westlet and Dad sit to the right. The press crowds the wide steps and soak her in with the kind of adoration Dad commanded before the Blight.

Do you want me on my knees? Because I will beg.

No. Not now, not ever. We are our House, and our House stands. Lord Westlet says he isn't heartless—and I'll hold *him* to *that*.

The Lady weaves history in bowstrings. I am love made flesh and bone. Eagle the Special Guard hero who sacrificed life and limb during a disaster relief mission. We met by chance on a border station between our Houses, and began a friendly correspondence that bloomed into beauty. Apparently Dad's newsfeed lockdown didn't extend to high-level military communication satellites, and since Eagle's the Heir and I'm a Daughter we were able to hack channels and sneak messages. We wrote constantly while he recovered. I'm what brought him back to life.

If starlight has a voice, it is Lady Westlet's.

Eagle shifts beside me. "Reggie's the hacker, Mother."

"Reggie?" I ask.

He focuses on the crowd, hands on knees.

I inch closer. "Is he the Electorate?"

"Really?" he asks. Disgust and disbelief.

Because obviously I should know already. Should have looked it up on the digislate Emmie only brought me this morning that can't connect to a network. Allotted research time somewhere between getting married and breaking the universe.

"Is Reggie here?"

No acknowledgment.

"You may not have to make him happy, but if he's Electorate then I *do*. Which one is he?"

"*They*. Reggie isn't Electorate, not yet, and he's not here."

"Children, there are cameras," says a melodic Lord Westlet from across the empty chair. "I suggest you smile."

Faithful, I am faithful.

I focus on the simmering Lady Westlet. Ignore the almost tangible drill of Dad's irritation.

"And now *you're* glaring," Lord Westlet says in singsong. I'm smiling, but I smile wider until my face near breaks. Then the Lord adds, "Let's try taking her hand, shall we?"

Eagle. He means Eagle.

I shift my left hand closer to his right, palm up. He doesn't move. Face forward, jaw set, biotech fingers impaling his knees. I'd pry them up, but the cameras would notice.

"Eagle," says his father in the exact tone as Dad's glare.

"I'm not contaminated anymore," I say. "I did the full round like everyone else. You can ask Dad."

"What?" Eagle asks.

"If you wouldn't mind sparing us a second?" asks the Lady, who has turned from the crowd to face us. "Your public wants to meet you."

Eagle stands in one swift motion, crosses in front of me and holds his left hand out. The real one.

Maybe he's wasn't worried about contamination.

I reach out, but Lady Westlet adds in an undertone, "Both, dearest."

Eagle stiffens. Wants to kill something.

I hold out both hands and he latches on. The Lady grins and slides close, lips brushing my cheekbone as she deftly detaches Eagle's good grip and pushes me into his right side.

"Like this." She pushes us into the spotlight.

The press doesn't grill us. No one asks, *And how did you hack a super secret, high-level military satellite exactly?*, or, *So did you ever visit him in the medicenter? Even once?* Instead they smile and I smile and Eagle sort-of-glares, and it's easy to fall into a rhythm of offering answers everyone thinks they already know.

"That is quite the gift," says a sturdy man near the front, his felt hat tipped askew over red hair. "How'd he earn it?"

"Gift?" I ask.

"The silver honor medal on your scarf, or do you wear it so often you forget?"

I reach for the pin. The clip *is* a medallion—molded wings and etched leaves like the valor medals at home. Rarely given and only for the hardest things that cost the most.

And Lady Westlet stuck it on my head as if it was some throwaway ribbon.

I grab its smooth edges, ready to yank. Except waxy fingers cover mine.

"Don't," breathes Eagle in my ear.

I turn and my nose brushes his. He's bent down that far, leaned that close.

"But it's in my *hair*."

"We're making them happy, remember?" There's something in his face, curling raw through his eyes, and I don't know if it's for me or the medal. "Leave it."

I let go.

"You didn't know?" the man asks. I jump. Everyone is full of knowing smiles, like we're the embodiment of kinetic hope.

Me and Eagle.

EMMIE IS RIGHT. DAD STAYS OFF MY BACK. HE LEAVES
without saying goodbye.

"Get anything of value?" Lady Westlet asks her flipcom,
curls agitated by her long, pacing steps. She's circled the
office eight times, past the framed glowering landscapes
and the orange-silver tapestries hanging overhead.

Lord Westlet leans against the heavy desk, ankles
crossed, shoes shiny black ravens on the pale carpet. "If he
did, it'd be a miracle."

The Lady glares, but he doesn't notice. He hasn't looked
at anything but me since the Lady herded us into his office.

I sit on the very edge of the wood chair. Hands on my
lap, shoulders back, toes curled tight.

Eagle's somewhere, behind me, maybe, or by the door.

The Lady cocks her head, then returns to the desk—
leaning behind Lord Westlet to grab a small black remote.
"Yes, I'm loading it now."

She points at one of the landscapes, and its moody purple mountains dissolve into a digital wall-screen. She scrolls
through menus and folders and loads the one she wants.

The picture fills the frame.

A boy in profile, scars hidden from view, leans close to a
girl who stares up like he's the only soul in the world. He's
touching her hand, the light is warming her skin, and any
moment now he'll kiss her—or maybe he just did.

They look so happy.

I feel sick.

Dawn breaks over Lady Westlet's face. "Everywhere. I want this everywhere. What price did we agree on? Never mind, double it. And clear your schedule—I do not care what it takes, this is your pet project from now on. Understood? Excellent. I'll send their itinerary."

She drops the flipcom on the desk and mirrors her husband's stance. "Your miracle, my lord."

Prickles skitter down my neck, build cities under my skin.

I am desperate to spring, to lunge for the remote and erase any and all trace of that shiny girl with my face who's happy and loved and hasn't broken anything.

Eagle watches the Lady. "Itinerary?"

"Detailed." Lady Westlet winks, then pushes off the desk. "But nothing too drastic. A few trips to the port, an event in the city—something low-key, a club maybe—and, of course, she'll join you on your walks. All of them, morning and evening. One of your many, mutual enjoyments."

"And you will hold hands," Lord Westlet adds to his son. "The entire time. In fact, anytime you are outside these walls. As far as the orderlies are concerned, you eat, sleep, and breathe together."

"Should we also make passionate love in the woods?"

asks Eagle with no emotion at all. I sink deep in my chair.

The Lord smiles. "It wouldn't hurt."

Eagle might be joking. His father isn't.

Lady Westlet sighs. "And have half-naked pictures of our future Lady popping up on the feeds? Really, dear, show some foresight."

"The Heir *was* our foresight. Our one justification to make this alliance tenable. And now?" Lord Westlet flicks a hand at me. "This."

I grip the edge of my seat. Force my eyes up to meet theirs.

Except Lady Westlet picks at her sleeve while Eagle maps the carpet.

"Eagle," says the Lady. "I think now would be an excellent time for a walk."

EAGLE'S FINGERS BARELY GRASP MINE. HE CUTS A straight line through the House complex, ignoring the interconnecting stone pathways that tangle without leading anywhere. There's no grid, no order to the lazy spirals and flowerbeds. The cluster of curved, half-moon towers are planted like haphazard trees. Sugary florals tangle with acrid needle bushes until my nose is dizzy from the mishmash. I'm lost in ten minutes, but Eagle never breaks pace. Another ten minutes and we reach the smallest tower on the very edge, set apart from the others. Nondescript. Without soul.

Eagle opens the door.

"Did you live here? Before I came?" I ask.

"No."

I didn't think so.

He lets me go as soon as we're inside. Once the elevator pings open, he's out of the lift and across the room.

"Eagle?"

He stops, hand on his door.

"Who are the Electorate?"

He glances at the Lady's scarf. "Didn't your father explain it?"

"Probably. To Emmie." I pull off the scarf, unpin the shiny medal with its silver leaves. Step forward and hold it out. "I told you. He didn't know."

He shakes his head and enters his room.

My hand tightens on the medal, but I don't throw it through the window or even at the couch—which is close and safe and wouldn't hurt it. Much.

Instead, I wrap the medal in the scarf and lay it on an end table.

Eagle's door reopens and he holds out a wide blue digislate—much nicer then the tiny gray one Emmie had. Heavier, too, screen glowing with images and text.

"The Electorate," he says and closes the door.

"IF IT WASN'T A TRICK, THEN WHY HASN'T FANE ENDED HIS blackout?" asks the elegant brunette, smooth voice over-high from the digislate's speakers. It's "Dravers" of *Finch and Dravers*—a commentary news program that most of the other network feeds refer back to, and seems to be everyone's favorite.

Finch raises bushy eyebrows—disheveled wrinkles to her polished charm. *"You mean in the three days since their union?"*

Two days. And a half, counting this morning.

The living room couch smells like it was unwrapped last week, but it's still much more comfortable than the desk chair in my room. And this way Eagle can see me and the slate and knows I'm not stealing it. It is right here and he can have it back whenever he wants.

He just has to ask first.

"For thirteen years we've had no trade, no contact—and now he has our Heir, *while his youngest daughter will be our future Lady."* Dravers shakes her head. *"How is that acceptable?"*

"He offered his Heir," Finch says mildly. *"And even the youngest Fane has only the Heir and Lord to contend with. As opposed to, say, a conclave?"*

The Electorate.

At home, Dad is power, but here power is spread about.

Governance is a collaborative effort between several families. Lord and Lady Westlet don't seem to rule as much as mediate—though they have power enough to seal a blood bond in secret, and it must have been secret because everyone was blindsided. Or pretending to be.

"Electorate" isn't an official title or office. It's about money. Who controls what industry, who married who when. If Miss Manufacturing Mogul is still talking to the Lord of Textiles, or if this up-and-coming financial mastermind is really the illegitimate son of that agricultural power. Who could devastate which particular aspect of the economy, and by how much. Most can't decide whether or not they like each other, let alone Lord and Lady Westlet. The only person they all seem to get on with is Eagle's younger brother, Regamund. Or Reggie-the-hacker-who-isn't-Electorate.

The elevator pings and Lady Westlet materializes.

"Surely you can't begrudge our future Lord the love of his life?" pips Finch, and I reach for the sound buttons on the digislate's side.

"When it means placing personal gratification over our future prosperity? Yes, I—"

I switch the slate off and dump it on the cushions. Drop my feet to the floor, my hands to my lap, and sit up straight. "Good morning, my Lady."

Nothing about her grim mouth says *good morning* back. She scans the room, then yells "Ea-*gle*," high enough my ears fizz.

I sink deeper into the couch.

"No, you don't, my girl." The Lady snaps her fingers, points, lifts. "Up."

I scramble to my feet as Eagle's door opens. He's got his scary look on—nondescript black clothes that fade into his skin and make the scars scream murder. "Yes?"

The Lady tips her head. "Ah, so you *are* here. Wasting away indoors when it's *such* a beautiful day. Perfect walking weather, don't you think? Especially when I am paying no small fee to have Jeffers and his camera wandering the grounds."

They could be talking about the weather. The kind with hail and sleet.

"It's on the itinerary," prompts Lady Westlet.

Eagle blinks from me to the digislate to his mom and doesn't say a word.

Oh.

"Verbal communication, darling," says the Lady. "I hear it's all the rage."

"I stole his digislate," I say.

The Lady leans back on her heels, and suddenly I'm the center of the world.

"I don't have one anymore?" My voice slides up an octave, and I try to pull it back. "So I stole his."

Eagle closes his eyes.

The Lady floats closer, glitter and sunshine. "Then I suggest you either keep up with his missives or give it back." She circles behind to press me toward Eagle. "Walk."

FAMILY

"M'LORD!" MARKEN, THE HOUSE GARDENER, runs up between the knotty vines and tangled trees, his frame twice mine and Eagle's together. "M'lady!"

I stop and so does Eagle, our loosely knit fingers stretching in the peppered sunlight. Our hands are back to back, the last two fingers woven. Touching as little as possible without seeming to, which makes the Lady happy.

Marken stops, a little winded but not much. "My Lord is looking for you both."

I wince. Eagle doesn't, but then his hood swallows everything so it's impossible to tell.

"We should have walked through the stickybells instead," I say. "I knew she'd find out."

Marken's lips twitch as he nods at a fuzzy green patch on the nearest tree trunk. "You mean that you sussed out the Lurker's allergy to the moss? I think My Lady already knows."

The Lurker being Lady Westlet's miracle photographer, who has lived in our shadow the past week because he has his very own itinerary, which exactly matches ours.

"Actually," Marken continues, shamefaced, "everybody knows. You have been walking this particular path morning, noon, and night."

"Only night and morning," I point out. "Noons are for fittings."

My clothes aren't pretty enough or stylish enough, and all much too Fane. Not to mention my hair. The Lady hates my hair.

Marken tips his head, bangs half in his eyes, smile hovering out of sight. "I'll tell my Lord you're on your way?"

"Yes," says Eagle. "Thank you."

Marken nods and rumbles back up the path and we're alone.

"Maybe he has other allergies," I say.

"Unlikely." Eagle sighs.

EAGLE OPENS THE DOOR TO THE LIBRARY AND THE light fractures. Stained-glass windows soar up and around the wide circular room, each peopled and landscaped in colors I can't even name.

"Impressive, aren't they?" says a lazy, liquid voice.

I focus past the color.

Lord Westlet sits amid a cluster of armchairs, under a window with an eagle cresting a full moon.

The real Eagle stands near the center of the room. "You sent for us?"

Lord Westlet waves his glass at the nearby chairs. The wine barely rocks. "Please, sit."

Eagle does. I don't.

Lord Westlet curls two beckoning fingers. "Come now, child. I won't bite."

He pats the armrest of the chair closest to his. I step slowly forward and sit.

"Better," says Lord Westlet. "Now, how would you like to fly home for the day? Visit the sister you gave up so much for?"

"Wren?" I scoot to the edge of the chair despite the sarcastic undertone.

Routines are important for coma patients, and I haven't seen Wren in over a week. Of course I told her goodbye so she knows why I'm gone, but—

But.

The Lord leans back in his seat and crosses his legs. "Of course, Eagle will go with you. And it won't be an extended family visit—the Lady wants you back tomorrow bright and early for your morning stroll—but there should be time enough to see your sister."

"My grandparents are dead," I say.

He blinks. "I'm sorry?"

"They only had Dad, and we don't speak to my mother. Dad and Emmie are my extended family."

His expression freezes, and relaxes twice as fast. "Then there will be no need to trouble either of them."

"You don't want Fane to know," says Eagle.

"You mean you wish to become better acquainted with your father-in-law?" Lord Westlet shakes his head. "Besides, I assumed you would rather see your sister."

More than anything.

"I won't do anything to her." I clutch the seat, look back and forth between them. "Whatever you're planning. I don't care."

He sighs. "Child, I have no designs on your sister."

"Then what are they on?" asks Eagle.

The Lord cuts him a Look. "That is not helpful."

Eagle doesn't answer and doesn't back down.

"Don't you want to see your beloved's homeworld?"

Lord Westlet's glass thuds to the table. "Really, Eagle, this is—" He catches my eye, shakes his head. "Something your mother will handle. You will fly to Fane and be back by tomorrow, and that is the end of it."

"Why?" Me. My voice, my question.

"*He* is my son," says Lord Westlet, "but you are not my daughter. Do not think this extends to you."

"Why?" Eagle repeats.

Lord Westlet's expression evaporates into nothing. He slowly refocuses on Eagle and leans even farther back.

The walls press close and heavy, and there's absolutely no doubt where Eagle gets his stare.

"I want you to locate Mekenna's husband," says Lord Westlet.

Pictures and articles shuffle through my head. I read about a Mekenna. It's not easy to tell who's Electorate and who isn't, but if it's Mekenna Solis, then she definitely is. She controls the greater half of Westlet's biotech manufacturing. She's also one of the few who seems to back the House family.

"Wouldn't that break the treaty?" Eagle shoots back.

His father nods toward me. "More than she has already?"

"I'm right here," I say.

He sighs. "We know that, dear. We live with it every day."

I straighten. "I do everything you ask."

"And you will do this." Lord Westlet's fluidity returns as he reaches for his glass. "Several of our people were trapped in Fane when your father initiated his lockdown. Orrin was there to visit your rainbow waterfalls, which I do hope were stunning since they cost him thirteen years. I want to know if he lives, how he lives, and how difficult it would be to retrieve him should it become necessary."

All it takes is one, Asa. One person, one word, one leak, and our lockdown is busted. Galton will know exactly how easy we'd be to invade.

The Lord watches over his bubbly wine, but the only voice in my head is Emmie's.

"But he could tell everyone about the Blight and the shortages," I say. "Galton would know."

"I guarantee that will not happen."

"Like you guaranteed our food?"

The Lord raises an eyebrow. I can't hold his stare like Eagle can, but every time I look away I look back.

"Do this," Lord Westlet says at last, "and at the end of the month when Fane sends the energy schematics, you'll have the rest of the initial shipment. Otherwise, your House will not see a single crate."

EAGLE'S FLIGHTWING ISN'T AS BIG OR SLEEK AS Wren's, but it moves faster. Or Eagle moves faster in it. We're off-planet in half an hour. Lord Westlet had contacted the border station before we even reached the library, and allotted Eagle enough fuel to get us home and back. We can't refill on Malsa, I don't have the energy tokens. Ecoflux isn't rationed, and it won't work in uleum engines.

Above the console gauges, stars fill the black beyond the viewshield. An embedded yellow screen follows our tiny blinking dot amid an expanse of stationary ones—less now than earlier. Westlet is double our size and defines most of our border, except for the far east sector where Galton space curves past Westlet to touch us.

Canaline, our last fuel-mineable planet, was in the east sector. We lost both it and the sector when Mom surrounded the planet with Galton war-carriers. Dad had to pull back our borders.

Void fills the wing inside and out. Eagle hasn't said anything since we took off.

But then, neither have I.

He taps the console screen and the map disappears in favor of the countdown sequence that will jump us into the Spacial Acceleration Zone. I hate SPAZing. Wren says it's impossible to *feel* the dimensional shift as we pop in and out of mind-melting speeds, because it only lasts a second.

A second where the universe hyperventilates at speeds that shouldn't exist.

The numbers on the console slip from three to two to one. The viewshield flashes white for a heartbeat, and then the stars change. Turn brighter, bluer, the frostlark belt a starry, weaving backdrop as we move toward the cloud-soaked, purple and green perfection of Malsa.

My Malsa.

The comlink flashes white above the console screen, and Eagle hits the button.

"Identity Code?" demands a gravel-ridden voice that promises oblivion if we don't answer immediately.

Casser could have gone anywhere after Urnath—Dad gave him a medal—but he said after eight months of quarantine and another six of evacuations, flight coordinator was about his speed.

Eagle opens his mouth, but I jump in first. "Zero one, five zero six cadalin."

"M'lady?" Casser explodes so loudly even Eagle sits back. "What are you doing off-planet?"

My greeting sticks in my throat.

"Off-planet," Eagle repeats. Or rather growls. "They think you're *on-planet*?"

"M'lady?" asks Casser in a wholly different tone.

Eagle knocks his head against the seat.

But Casser has to know I'm married. On Urnath he always knew everyone's secrets, and our alliance with Westlet is definitely not a secret.

Unless Dad made it one.

"M'lady," Casser repeats, "is everything all right?"

"Yes."

No, not remotely.

And Casser knows it. "Right. Of course. Didn't they update your identity code a while back? Aren't you a two two nine yellow?"

Two two nine yellow. The Urnath base distress code, for when flight crews coasted in on fumes—their engines blown or out of fuel. Which was every flight, near the end. Casser always wanted to know where Wren found fuel to send them out, when he was absolutely positive we had no uleum left. And every time Wren would sigh explanations that made perfect sense.

And that weren't true.

He's going to figure it out, I said.

No, he won't. Wren folded her arms on her desk and dropped her head there. *Not if the story's good enough.*

And he didn't.

I just need a story.

"I—" Come on, Asa, *think.* "I wanted to see Urnath, so

Eagle took me. I told him I had Dad's permission, so Eagle thought he knew. Don't tell Dad, okay? We didn't land or anything, just flew by."

"Eagle?" asks Casser.

Eagle's eyes narrow, the shiny ridges of his cheek catching in the light.

"We went through Decontamination together," I say.

Casser's gruffness turns woolly soft. "I know they dusted the planet, m'lady, but that's no place to be wasting fuel flying by."

"I know, but the sun doesn't rise the same way anywhere else. Not all purple-orange gray."

"That was just the city haze. Lucky we weren't all sick even before the Blight."

"Yeah, but don't you miss it?"

"Every damn day." He sighs. "Get on home with you then. My Lord won't hear it from me."

RYSSEL ISN'T THE BIGGEST CITY IN FANE OR EVEN ON Malsa, but it glows. Ad-screens wink from skytowers as we fly through the clouds. I plug the medicenter's coordinates into the console, and Eagle weaves through the scattered traffic like he was born here. There isn't much, a few transit flight-buses between the bright neon of the new ecoflux wings. No one has rations enough to fly on uleum anymore, and Dad had to stop new wing production during the Blight.

It's been forever since the skies were full.

In ten minutes or so, I'll get to see Wren.

The medicenter's docking bay could house the Westlet complex's main tower and then some—airy gray with multi-tiered platforms. I direct Eagle to one near the coma ward's floor. He sets down, powers off. The engine's low hum slowly dies, until it's just us and the viewshield and the long steel wall staring in.

"You were—"

"I didn't—"

The quiet crawls.

I should probably go first. I don't want to. He must not, either.

"It's only been a week," I say. "I'm sure Dad's going to tell everyone once everything's settled and stable, but with lockdown he's probably worried that people would want to leave for Westlet."

And they'd have a right to. Because we're allies and blood bonded and everyone else in the Triplicate can go and come as they like.

All week the Lady has paraded us everywhere for pictures Eagle hates because his fingers flinch every time he sees a camera.

Dad hasn't even told my House that Eagle exists.

"Together," he says.

I look up. "What?"

His arms are taut, hands on the steershift. "You said we went through Decontamination *together*."

"Casser was Wren's second on base. I couldn't say I knew you in quarantine because Casser knew everybody I knew in quarantine. And, well, everyone else. But during Decontaimination it was just me and Wren, so he wouldn't know you weren't there."

"You were in the Blight that destroyed your planet?"

"Well, yes?"

Everyone knows that.

I thought everyone knew that.

Nothing in Eagle's searching eyes says he knew that.

"I'm not contaminated anymore," I say. "They made sure." Double sure, keeping us an extra week while Wren's scans deteriorated and her heart almost stopped. Twice.

Eagle starts to say something but we're *here*, home, wasting time in a stupid flightwing talking about stupid things when Wren's within walking distance and wondering where I am.

I get up, grab my daypack from under the chair, and press open the cockpit door. "Wren's waiting."

I SHOULD HAVE STOLEN EAGLE'S HOOD. WE'RE stopped three times in four minutes. Nara, Gregor, Kelie— all the coma ward medics who have seen me almost every day, and for a week haven't seen me at all.

"I'm so glad you're well, m'lady." Nara squeezes my hand, scalp glistening under the short blonde fuzz of her hair, laugh lines deep and sunny even post-quarantine. She smiles up at Eagle's hood as if she can penetrate its shadow. "We normally set our clocks by her."

The hood zeros in on me, but I ignore him. "How is Wren?"

"Good, good, though they're rerunning all the probability tests on her again. A multilevel diagnostic."

"Her monitor spiked?"

"I wouldn't know about that," Nara says slowly. "You know how Aston is about patient information. Though maybe, it would make sense, it's just with them rolling her off to diagnostics the first day you're off-schedule—"

"Is she there now? Do we need to go?" I bounce, ready to bolt back down the hall.

If she's in diagnostics, I'll only see her through the window. She won't even know I'm here.

If they're retesting, Dad must have listened about the mountains.

"No, no, m'lady," Nara says. "She's in her room. She's

fine, everything's fine." To prove it, she launches into a full detail of Wren's care as we walk the tiled hall.

The medicenter's wards have themes, and this unit is Stormy Beaches. Speckled blue floor with painted waves, clinical gray walls crowded with doors and security panels, flecked yellow-gray ceiling. Stinging antiseptic mixes with the bright florals from puffpetals potted on the central reception desk.

We've almost reached Wren's door when another voice calls, "Is that m'lady? Is she well?"

"Yes, very well it looks like," Nara calls back over her shoulder. "She just got herself a boy."

I sink into my hoodless, unhelpful jacket and press my palm to Wren's security scanner.

"It was good to see you." I smile at Nara, and all but push Eagle through the door. Only Wren's dedicated specialists have room access. Everyone else needs permission from Dad or Emmie or me. The door clicks shut behind us.

Wren sleeps amid crisp sheets, backlit by sunset and birdsong.

I drop my bag and rush to the bed, grabbing the handrail before I run into it. I take her limp, cool hand between both of mine and hug it close. "Hey, Wren."

Her baby-pink lips don't twitch and her lashes don't flutter and the monitor *beep beep beeps* its normal, steady rhythm. I lay my forehead against hers. "Hey."

My voice only slips a little, and my eyes are barely even wet. She smells like the white onnil soap I asked the medics to special order because it was her favorite.

"Did you miss me?"

Low, steady breath.

"Well, that figures. You were probably having too much fun, right? And Aston's been feeding the birds! I left all that seed so you should be set for a while. And this is—"

Except Eagle isn't by the bed. He's at the door, only a few steps inside. I wave him closer.

Hesitant, near silent footfalls. Eagle stops at the end of the bed, hands in pockets.

"This is Eagle," I say. "Eagle, Wren."

"Hello," he says. Not baby sweet, but straightforward. As if Wren was awake as anybody.

Which ties so many knots inside it hurts.

"She can't see you," I tell him.

He pushes off his hood, but looks at me. A weird, steady look that pulls every which way and knocks the quiet out of sync.

I focus on Wren. Or rather her hand, which I'm squeezing tight. Too tight. I lay it on the bed. Except now my fingers have nothing to do.

"Your father really didn't know," Eagle says and the

truth's there. Touchable. The whole scope of it. Not just Dad knowing, but me choosing. And here we are, for one precious hour with my sister, and he just keeps watching *me*.

I slide back from the bed and him and reach for the bag I dropped. My digislate is tied to Fane's seal with print-scan access for most things, which should work now that I'm at home. "I'll find Orrin."

"WHAT ARE THE TESTS FOR?" I ASK.

For all of Aston's wild hair and his half-buttoned coat, he can turn into a human wall when he wants to. Rather like Eagle, who stands at the window with his hood back up.

"Standard procedure, m'lady," Aston says. "Nothing to worry you."

Aston is forever concerned about my anxiety level.

"I'm not worried," I say. "I want to know what they're *for*."

"A routine check of her current cognizance levels."

"And on whose authority? Emmie's or Dad's?"

My digislate beeps on the bed by Wren's feet. I reach down, save the latest match, and reinitiate the scan one-handed. It has beeped three times thus far, and none of the pictures resembled the burly man Lord Westlet gave us. I have access to most of the upper-level civic House networks, but my slate doesn't have the processing speed of Wren's old one—especially when running simultaneous scans for name and facial match.

"The scan order has the lead specialist's signature," Aston says. "As I explained, m'lady, this is all routine. No need for concern."

"Then why did they start once she left?" asks Eagle from the window. I didn't think he was listening.

Aston waves him away. "This is a House matter, sir."

"Eagle is House," I say.

"M'lady—"

"No." I glance at the wall digiclock. We're running out of time. Lord Westlet's waiting, and even with Casser's silence, the border station would have told Dad I'm in Fane. He might come looking. "I want Wren's blood."

Aston's jaw drops. "M'lady?"

"For transport. Three vials at least, and all of her scans and diagnostics. Everything."

Which should be enough for Westlet medics to run tests of their own, once I can track down some specialists.

The digislate beeps, and I *tap tap tap*.

"M'lady," says Aston, baby sweet. "I don't think that's wise. Everything's under control. There's nothing to worry about."

Just because I'm not Dad or Wren doesn't mean I'm not me.

"This *is* a House matter," I say, slow enough that the syllables march. "I want my sister's records. Now."

His shoulders drop and I almost take it back.

But it's about Wren, so I don't.

"As you say, my lady." He nods once and disappears through the door.

And Wren can't be getting any better, because if she was she would sit up and say, *well, wasn't that well done?*

"I don't want to hear it," I say.

"I didn't say anything," says Eagle.

"I wasn't talking to you."

The hood swings back toward the city, and I wrap my hands behind my neck. Wrong, everything, all of it. And one hour with Wren is not enough.

"Blood?" Eagle asks.

"For your medi-specialists, so they can make her a new medichip. Her old one always kept her safe before."

"Fane has medichips?"

I shake my head. "No, you gave it to us. I mean, your last Lord gave it to Dad. Lord Westlet's older brother." He died before I was born—a bad fever.

Eagle nods, hands deep in his pockets.

"You're chipped, right?" I ask.

A half beat of stillness, then he marches toward the bed like we're back in Westlet. "Did you get a match?"

"But you are. You have to be. You're the Heir. It's your biotech."

He lifts my digislate, scans the search data speeding across the screen. "Where are the matches?"

"You didn't take it out." I snatch the slate and hug it to my chest. "Why would you take it out? Tell me you didn't take it out."

"What do you care?" He reaches for the slate but I back up.

118

"Are you chipped?"

"*Yes.*"

"*Good.*"

"*Matches.*" Eagle crosses his arms like *good* is what everything isn't.

But it is, because if there are bombs and he gets caught in the crossfire, he'll wake up.

I suspend the digislate's current search to load the files saved so far. Swipe through this name and that face. Wrong age, wrong gender, wrong coloring.

Then there he is, Orrin Solis. Square jawed with small, smug eyes.

"Oh," I say.

Eagle doesn't move as much as deflates. "He's dead."

I shake my head. "He's married."

"I know."

"No, I mean *here.*" I step close so he can see the screen with Orrin's status ID coupled with connected newsfeed articles I had set up the search to include. Like the *New Restaurant Opening* feature from a small city two planets over, with a beaming family outside a skytower shop front. Orrin, his lithe pretty wife, and their freckled ten-year-old son.

"Oh," says Eagle.

TRUTH

WALK WITH MY EYES CLOSED. EAGLE MUST BE TIRED, too, because we don't march through the dewy hedge garden. We flew in around dawn with maybe two hours of sleep, before Lord Westlet requested us.

The Lord took one look at my slate with its picture, and sent us on our walk.

"Wake up," says Eagle.

"I am awake."

His tone deepens. "Someone's ahead."

"If it's the Lurker, I don't care." But I rub the sleep from my eyes.

Footsteps crunch ahead where the path twists, and a boy appears around the bend. Westlet-tall with a broad smile. "Why, if it isn't my favorite brother!"

Eagle stops so fast I end up a step ahead of him. "You're home," Eagle says.

The boy—it has to be Reggie—raises a tapered brow above wide, clear eyes. "Disappointed?"

Eagle lets the word hang, so I jump in with, "Of course he isn't."

Reggie steps forward, sliding my fingers from Eagle's to take both my hands. "And you must be the latest addition to our little family." He pulls my arms up and out for inspection, then kisses my knuckles. "Quite charming."

His mouth lingers and I want my hands back.

"It's a pleasure," he says, like he actually means it.

Eagle is a monolith, sucking out Reggie's light.

Reggie lets go and offers a hand to his brother. His right hand, not his left. "Eagle."

Dad once said the entire universe can be conveyed in the timing of a handshake. Eagle waits long enough to notice, then accepts Reggie's hand before it falls.

They're the same height, even the same build. But Reggie has Lord Westlet's high cheeks without the symmetry, his mother's skin without its near black depth.

Smooth skin, no scars.

"Regamund." Eagle lets go, then reaches for me with his real hand. Not just reaches—slides all his fingers in the spaces between mine until our palms press tight. Fused skin and sure fingers generating warmth that echoes all the way up. I stare at our hands.

Eagle watches his brother.

Reggie steps aside and waves us down the path with an elegant flourish. "I see I've interrupted your walk. Mustn't keep you."

Eagle takes off, and I jog to keep up.

"Nice to meet you," I call over my shoulder.

Reggie bows. "Just the first of many introductions, I'm afraid."

Eagle stops dead. "What?"

But now Reggie is moving, walking backward down the path. "Why, the cousins, of course. They'll be here for breakfast."

"Which ones?" asks Eagle.

Reggie shrugs. "Oh, Elona, and Charles I expect, and perhaps even his effervescent mother. One can only hope." He saunters away.

Eagle watches, hand still wrapping mine.

I shake his palm until he turns. "What's wrong with the cousins?"

"Electorate. Charles is Mekenna's son."

Oh.

"CHILDREN!" LADY WESTLET FLOATS DOWN THE veranda steps, a bubble of long arms and pink white lace. She reaches up to kiss my cheek, then stands on tiptoe for Eagle. Adds in an undertone, "Your father wants you."

"Did he invite them?" Eagle asks, but the Lady shakes her head.

"That would be your brother. Apparently after his snow-skidding adventure tour of Barhelna, he spent a few days with Mekenna, who suggested a visit."

"And Reggie agreed."

"Be nice. Mekenna is one supporter we *cannot* lose. He could hardly say no. And speaking of—" The Lady leans past Eagle's shoulder and waves dancing fingers. "Reggie, darling! Come meet your new sister."

"I've already had that honor," Reggie calls from up the walk, hands in his pockets, lean elbows spread wide with his languid steps.

"Have you?" asks the Lady. "Then the question becomes, have you taken her riding?"

"No," says Eagle.

The Lady sighs. "Interestingly enough, she *is* her own person. You do not get to dictate her movements."

"You do," I say.

She doesn't miss a beat. "I'm your mother-in-law, that's another thing entirely." She pats Eagle's cheek, deftly splits our hands, and pulls me down the path to Reggie. Greets him with the same kiss she gave Eagle.

"Reggie, do be a dear and look after Asa for me? It would be good for her to have a few practice flights before the cousins monopolize her time in the stables. Besides, your brother is on tirade."

Reggie returns the kiss. "Is he ever off tirade?"

"Eagle doesn't tirade," I say, for which I get Looks.

"Well," Reggie weaves my arm through his, pats my hand. "I guess they did circumvent a blood bond together. Daric was almost apoplectic when he heard, though I'm not sure if it was for that or the treaty itself."

Daric is Lord Westlet's first cousin, and even more Electorate than Mekenna, judging by the newsfeeds. He seems to have the closest blood tie to the Westlets, and the least goodwill.

"Yes," says the Lady, drawing out the word. "Poor Daric. With him, apoplexy is a state of being. And I'm much afraid your brother will inherit the habit." She smiles light and feathers and waves us away. "So, off with you. Enjoy the skies."

with *wings*. Actual wings that flitter and fill the stable stalls around their barrel bodies and tree-trunk limbs.

Giflons. I've seen pictures in some of the old feed articles at home while looking for medichips. I thought the writers were making them up.

A smushed orange face snorts stale heat, and I freeze, hand halfway to its nose. The stable is almost as large as a public docking bay, each stall wide enough to land a small flightwing. Or a massive giflon.

"Are you real?" I ask.

Its huge nose brushes wet pebbles against my fingertips, before it leans down and licks my ear. I yelp and jump back.

"Careful." Reggie reappears from a stall farther down, carrying a wide gray saddle. "Too much attention and she'll never leave you alone. Get the door, will you?"

I scramble to unhook the latch and open the stall. "We're not riding that, are we?"

"Her," Reggie corrects, throwing the saddle over its back. "And *we're* not, *you* are."

"By myself? But we don't have giflons in Fane."

"Don't worry. Panna's just a big kitten, and I'll be right beside you the whole way."

I retreat a step. The giflon looms until I swear her head

brushes the rafters, her slitted cat eyes hungry. "Maybe we could ride something else?"

Reggie laughs, slips from the stall and walks so close I back into one of the support posts. He leans in until I can see the purple in his irises. "Don't tell me that of all people, Fane's Daughter is *scared*."

Yes. Terrified. But that's not the right answer.

Most all of the Electorate like Reggie. He goes snow-skidding with them.

"No," I say. "I'm not scared."

"Oh, come now. I've heard you lie better than that." He brushes the hair off my ear with airy fingertips that frighten sparks down my neck.

"I haven't lied," I say.

"And what do you call stealing a blood bond?" Warm and teasing. "Universal truth?"

"Love." Sure, instant. True.

Wren needed me.

Reggie's smile falters. "Now that does sound suspiciously honest. Eagle must be quite the lucky boy."

No, not really.

Reggie returns to the stall, and suddenly it's easier to breathe. I sidestep the post so if he comes marching back there's more room to run.

"Does Eagle come flying a lot?" I ask.

Reggie grabs the reins and pushes the door wide open. "Forsake his precious wheels for a being with a heart and soul? Oh, constantly."

"Wheels?" I ask.

"His skidcycle."

"Skidcycle?"

Eagle? With his never-ending crisp suits and speed-walking nonconversation? A *skidcycle*?

"You mean you haven't seen it?" The giflon snuffles Reggie's shoulder, but he ignores her, puts his full focus on me. "Lord, I'd have thought that'd be the first thing he'd— didn't he write about it? In his letters?"

My heart fists tight.

Think, Asa, think it through.

Eagle has a *skidcycle*?

"Yeah." I squeeze my eyes, shake my head. "My sister loves engines so much, and it was all she would talk about. I got good at tuning her out, so whenever Eagle gets technical I don't even notice." I shrug, find a smile. "Sometimes habits are hard to break."

"Yes." For once, Reggie looks exactly like his brother. Unreadable. "They can be. Here, I'll help you up."

GIFLONS LOVE SKIMMING TREES. AND BUILDINGS. AND anything spiked or deadly. Swooping in and then away at the last possible second.

Like the main tower's storytelling windows.

I swallow a scream. Duck my head behind the giflon's ear and bury my hands in her fur.

"Easy there, Panna!" Reggie laughs from somewhere behind, but air whips and wings flap and my heart somersaults over my stomach while the giflon approaches another wall at full speed.

"Don't crash," I beg into the coarse grind of her fur. "Please, don't crash."

She snorts, flexes her massive shoulders and banks hard. My bones rattle and—

Don't flatten into the tower like a puffcake.

I peek one eye open. Both. Below us the ground rushes in a maze of paths and grass and windowed balconies with yanked open doors and people coming out.

"Eagle!"

He's there, right there, motionless on the balcony by his dad, craned neck and sun-soaked hair. Not tall, but tiny. Forever away.

Panna agrees. She dives toward him.

The planet tilts.

My foot slips and the stirrup disappears. No strap across

my toes, no fur at my ankle. Wind rips fury until my whole leg dangles. Air. Nothing but. Opposite knee skidding over the saddle's hump, until it's just me and the wind.

Slide slide sliding.

The upper corridor roars. Explodes. A fiery fist buckling the supply warehouse walls, throwing me back onto floor that isn't flat like it should be, but sloped and slide slide sliding. I bounce, skitter against tile as the floor gapes open to swallow me whole.

Wind snatches my voice. My ears ring, and my head.

Then the world levels. My leg slaps into fur and my stomach bottoms out. I clutch at reins and skin and—

—scrabble along the slick upper ramp. Screaming, everyone's screaming. Me, the soldiers, Wren. Who was somewhere below, with the rations crew. Closer to the blast. "Wren!" My feet hit the floor's busted edge and slide off.

Footsteps pound between wingbeats and screams. Dust and fur in my nose, under my nails.

"The rail, m'lady!" Casser thunders through the smoke. "Goddamn it, Asa, grab the rail!" I stretch, hand scraping the splintered support just as my back follows my feet off the ledge.

I bounce. Against the buckled corridor. Against a broad saddled back.

The wind stops and the world stills and I clutch the furry rail.

"Hold on, you hear me? Hold on."

"Asa." A hand tugs my foot. "Let go."

But that's wrong, I know that's wrong, and I kick it away.

"Asa—"

"I'mholdingI'mholdingonwhere'sWren?"

The hand stops tugging. "Safe. So are you."

I curl forward, hunch my shoulders.

"Asa." Weighted as Casser's boom. "Look up."

My head lifts automatically. There are no walls, no warehouse. Just blue and green. Sky and field. Bushes and—

"Eagle?"

He stands by my foot, fur all over his brown shirt, hand up and stretching. "Let go."

I do. Slowly, knuckle by knuckle, and reach down. He pulls my wrist until he can slide his hands under my arms, and lifts.

I'm on my feet. Steady level feet on steady level grass.

My ribs have gone hollow and glassy, and Eagle holds them together with all ten of his fingers.

"Okay?" he asks.

But there's smoke in my nose and the colors are too bright.

"Wren," I say.

Eagle bends so closely our foreheads almost touch. "She's all right."

"No, she's not. She's not at all."

Movement, then Reggie appears at our side. "Asa, are you—"

"Don't," says Eagle, and even the birds shut up. "Don't try that again."

"How was I to know Panna would bolt?"

But now Eagle ignores him for me. "Ready?"

I nod. He steps back, offers his arm instead of his hand. I wind mine through his. We walk back toward the complex as Reggie watches, one hand on Panna's mane.

FAITHFUL

BREAKFAST IS A CACOPHONY OF COUSINS. THEIR voices bounce off the arched ceiling, weave through the skylight's rays, rumble down the long wooden table with its army of chairs. Milky platters and crystal cups. Silverware etched with roots and leaves. Plates inlaid with gold filigree.

Breakfasts are formal in Westlet. It shows in the silver ribbons in the Lady's hair and the sea gray of Lord Westlet's cuffs. The Lord sits at the head of the table, watching the commotion with heavy bored eyes that never stray too far from me on his left.

Eagle is two chairs down and impossible to see without lying on my plate.

I try not to speak.

Mekenna Solis sits beside me. Long roped braids shift over her shoulder to brush mine as she converses with the Lord. She isn't lithe or blonde. Her chin is too narrow, her eyes too big and demanding, her ears overlarge and almost tipped. Strong, regal, but not pretty. Her son Charles takes after her, no lanky limbs and cute freckles. He doesn't look much like Orrin—the father who forgot his existence.

Maybe, in a few years, Dad will forget that I exist, too.

Mom did.

Wren wouldn't.

Mekenna catches me looking. Inclines her head. "So nice to finally meet our future Lady in person. She's quite the exotic butterfly."

"More like a screech beetle." Charles grins at me from her other side, gelled hair bobbing. Mekenna raps the back of his hand with her knuckle, and he subsides with a mumbled, "Sorry."

"A screecher, Charles?" Across the table, Elona West-let jangles her silver bracelets. And she *is* a Westlet, with all their static power. She is Daric's oldest, Eagle's second cousin, and sits across from me on the Lord's right. "She's almost as mute as Eagle."

"Likely most of the appeal." Reggie sits between Elona and the Lady, the only male without a suit, brown silk shirt unbuttoned at the top.

"Yes, *now*." Charles stabs enough eggs for three people. "You should have seen her yesterday. There's a holorecord."

The Lurker recorded that?

I cut my melon into smaller and smaller pieces. If I can get them into slivers, maybe I can swallow one without my stomach throwing it back.

"No, a holorecord?" Mekenna raises a glass to Lady Westlet, either an acknowledgment or a challenge. "Do tell."

"Yes! Do!" Elona hems the Lady in. "You must have a true artist on staff. Considering how the feeds follow their every move, it's amazing how little of Eagle we actually see. They always seem to catch his bearable side."

I scrape my fork on my plate. Loud even in the clatter.

"Oh, you wouldn't know, of course," Elona says to me, "but Eagle was once the prettiest boy in the family."

"I heard that," says Reggie.

Elona rubs his shoulder. "I said *was*. Pay attention."

"Is." I lay down my fork with care. "Is."

She laughs. Rich, bouncing notes.

I stare until they die.

Lord Westlet shifts in my peripheral.

"Asa, dear," says the Lady, "your eggs are getting cold."

"No, you're right," says Elona, smile hovering. "Why else would they marry him off in a blind irreversible ceremony to a locked down House who wouldn't know better? Can't have the House bloodline dying out due to all that *prettiness*."

My chair shreds the floor. I'm on my feet and towering, voice Dad-soft. "We know better. We know exactly what better means and what it looks like. How much it's worth. Eagle is everything better and I know especially, because

I have seen *worse*."

And right now *worse* is the tall girl with shattered grace and blood lips.

They better not move. I will eviscerate them if she even thinks about moving them.

"Asa," says Lord Westlet, in the exact same tone he had used to ask for the salt. "Wait for me in the library."

He tips his head, his eyebrows gentle arcs that don't mask the knives in his stare.

I open my mouth, but he carefully and deliberately slices the corner off his toast with a *click click*. He stabs the brown square and lifts it to the light. Examines the edge with a lazy twist. "I'm sorry, did that sound like a request?"

Mekenna eyes me like I'm a *very* exotic butterfly indeed, but Eagle doesn't eye me at all. On my feet I can see him—his head down, hands flat on the table. Preparing for the bomb that will ignite any second and hit him first.

Except there are no bombs here. Only sunshine, his family, and me.

I walk out.

I WAIT IN COLOR. MY DRESS TINTED BLUE AND GREEN from the windows. Sit across from Lord Westlet's chair. Eagle isn't here.

Behind me, the door opens. I am very still and straight. I haven't cried once.

And my cheeks can prove it.

A heavy feminine sigh. "What are we going to do with you?"

Lady Westlet weaves between the chairs. She drops into her husband's seat. "Of all the people *not* to humiliate. Elona lives for retribution. Charles would have been a better target, even with his mother there. Mekenna at least would be straightforward in her revenge."

"She said he was only half bearable." Shaky. Crinkled at the edges. Like me.

"That she did." The Lady leans forward, arms resting on her knees. "We are not Fane, Asa. Arron does not hold absolute power, not like your father. Your lockdown?" She shakes her head. "Well, I still don't know how he managed that particular feat even in Fane, but here it would be an impossibility. We are a collective. Our family, or rather my husband's, has only held House status since Arron's aunt Seraphina died and his father turned Heir. And Elona is the grandchild of that aunt. If Seraphina had lived, Elona would have Eagle's place. And there are many, a great many, who would have preferred that scenario. She knows it, her father knows it, and so do we."

Elona? As *Heir*?

The Lady shrugs a smile. "We walk a very fine line. Fane was never universally liked, and his lockdown not only severed trade but families. Most of the Electorate would rather see us dead then allied with Fane."

"Then why? Why us?"

She searches my face. "Do I have your silence? Your word as your father's daughter?"

A request, not a command.

"Yes."

"We need your fuel. We have perhaps two years of uleum left. Maybe three. Most of our reserves were destroyed during the meteor strike." Her bitterness creeps into resignation. "Eagle's, in fact."

Eagle's scars. The disaster relief mission. I almost looked it up, several times. Wanted to. But I only have Eagle's digislate for research. On mine it wouldn't matter, but on his it somehow does.

"You mean when he got his medal?"

"Yes, he was in training for the Guard during the strike. The planet will recover, but the pre-mined reserves are gone and even our populated planets are not as uleum-rich as yours. The Electorate is unaware, and it is absolutely imperative they remain so. Your father said you could not survive an invasion? We would not survive a revolt."

"You think they'd revolt?"

"Without a doubt. Not as a whole perhaps, but enough. Seraphina was much loved, and for good reason. And while I would say Arron retains more of Seraphina's goodness than her own offspring, not many would agree. Which is why we wanted the Heir. Having full proxy powers in your House, where Lordship means *complete* authority, would have soothed a great deal of feathers."

I can't meet her eyes. The armchair is small and I am smaller still.

I broke their family. I'm going to break their House.

"No, do *not* misconstrue me." She lifts my chin. "The majority of the Electorate wouldn't have approved of this bond even if we had your sister. And despite Arron's current feelings on the subject, I'm beginning to believe we may not have been entirely shortchanged in this arrangement, and should perhaps hold to our end of the bargain, if you learn to hold your tongue and pick your battles."

Her brown eyes spark, intent and depth, and I swallow hard.

"I'm sorry, my Lady, but I pick this one."

She sighs. "Let me rephrase. You will fight your battles with temperance and tact, in a way befitting the future Lady of this House. Which does not include standing over your second cousin and calling her repulsive scum."

"I didn't—"

"You thought it and trust me, we all knew." She straightens, shoulders back. "The Lord and I will not live forever and when you take our places, I promise you will face worse than this. Best to practice and prepare. This behavior cannot be repeated, is that clear?"

Light dances across the carpet, broken into colors that don't fit.

"Your word, Asa," says the Lady.

"You have it."

I BURY THE LIVING ROOM IN ORANGE-SPECKLED yellow. Marken, the gardener, didn't have any leftover nonspeckled paints. His shed was full of everything mismatched and unwanted. Apparently the best quality colors come from a small moon two planets over, owned by somebody's uncle's cousin's third husband, who had a tiff with somebody else's second niece, which the uncle's cousin found out about because prior to the tiff there had been an affair, and what with my Lord's new fuel rations on nonessential shipments, nobody in this system has had decent paint for six months.

Yellow smacks the wall and spatters into a dripping, dead sun. I smear it everywhere.

The elevator pings. Booted footfalls, then silence.

Paint rains over me and my feet and the drip sheet–covered floor. "If you hate it, Marken said he could probably track something else down next week, but it can't be white because everything's white and it's not even your color—it's mine."

Except Fane white hints at rainbows, while this white says nothing much.

Neither does Eagle. Of course he doesn't.

I slather on another coat, which colorbot paint wouldn't need, but this isn't Fane and there are no colorbots. Not that Dad ever let me paint anything at home.

On Urnath, Wren let me paint whatever I wanted. Except her biotech models, those were off-limits.

Eagle appears on my right. Not especially close, but not forever far. He has abandoned his suit jacket somewhere and rolled his left sleeve up to his elbow. Not the right, though, where the pale blue fabric is locked to his wrist and already flecked yellow. He dips the haggard backup brush into the color canister and smears the wall.

He works his way from middle to top, backtracking for drips and making more. After a minute, I stretch on my toes and paint as high as I can reach. I keep at it until he catches on and stretches, too—almost to the ceiling trim.

We find a rhythm. Him still in his breakfast clothes. Me in a work shirt from one of Wren's old uniforms. Fabric swishes and worn bristles. Wind sighs beyond the open balcony doors. It's weird only coming up to his shoulder. His arm is an impossibly long line from elbow to fingertips—orange-flecked and popberry-yellow and glistening from the work.

"It's not worth it," he says.

I jump and my brush zags. "What?"

"Elona. Next time, let it go."

"It's *wrong*," I say. "*She's* wrong, no matter who her grandmother was."

"But you didn't know." His glance is here and gone.

"I remember."

"I was supposed to be Emmie!"

"She didn't know, either. I saw her face."

Of course, she knew. Dad would have told her. Because Lord Westlet would have told him.

Except, Emmie never mentioned the burns, and she would have. She mentioned everything else.

"That has nothing to do with anything," I say.

His reply disappears behind his brush. He slathers the spot he just painted with a second coat. A third. A fifth.

"Even if she didn't know, that doesn't make it true."

Eagle leans in until I can count all the orange speckles flecked over his cheeks. It must have gotten in his eyes, too, because under all the black and lashes are hints of orange gold.

"You want your House to eat?" There's no threat in his face. Just fact.

"Yes."

"Let me handle them. Father was livid before, but at Fane. Not you." He switches the brush to his right hand and holds out his left, his palm as paint-sticky as my fingers, which are already somehow wrapped in his warm, tight grip. "Deal?"

"I already promised your mom I'd—"

"Deal?" Quiet and strong at once. Like the eyes that

won't leave me alone, saying we can stand here all day. Just like this. It's that important.

One.

Soft.

Shake.

TIMING IS EVERYTHING IN A HANDSHAKE. I FORGOT to count the seconds. I stare at the ceiling above my bed as my hand tingles and memory rewinds, but I didn't count the seconds and I don't know how many there were.

I AM A SCREECH BEETLE. I PANIC THROUGH THE DIGI-slate's speakers. Eagle is with his dad, and the Lady took the cousins. I have a full half hour alone to research specialists and medichips, and am even able to sneak under the upper study's half-moon desk which could hide whole armies.

And all I do is watch me.

Panna's huge furred wings beat and bank. Dive and stretch. Bloom into a long vertical line with me at the center, dangling. Left leg, torso, and most of my right thigh free-floating in the open air.

Falling.

It's not until the falling that I scream.

"Thought I heard something," says a voice, and I nearly jump out of my skin.

Reggie's head is half upside down as he peers under the desk. Even contorted he's the epitome of balance, one hand on the desktop. "Comfortable?"

I hold up the slate. Point to the distant floating Reggie in the corner of the frame. He never gets closer. I've watched it three times.

He doesn't even try.

"I'd like to be alone, please," I say with temperance and tact.

Reggie slides under the desk instead, head scraping the

grainy underside. "You know, before your arrival we could breathe without cameras."

I swipe the screen off, hold it balanced on my raised knees. "You wanted me to fall."

His smile doesn't change, but now there's paste holding it together. "Don't be dramatic."

I tap the screen back on, reload the image, and hold it out.

He doesn't take it.

"The blood bond exists without me," I say. "If you're trying to kill the treaty, my falling won't help."

Reggie settles back into the curve of the desk. "Not much of a dancer, are you?"

"Do you want proof?" I reactivate the slate and open a network search. "Blood bonds are—"

I start to rise, but he lays two fingers on my wrist. "I have been informed, in no uncertain terms, exactly how blood bonds work. Do spare me a second lecture." Then his fingers spider across my hand to the screen, and swipes through my recent search history.

I yank the slate away, but not before he reaches the one page I hadn't exactly meant to look up.

"The Special Guard?" asks Reggie. "I'd have thought you'd have enough of them, what with all those long, long love letters."

"We didn't talk about it."

"Really? It was all he talked about before."

Needles prick my skin, and I swear Reggie sees every puncture. I rise, but he takes my wrist. Again. "Tell you what, I'm a veritable font of Eagle information. I'll answer your questions if you answer mine."

"What questions?"

He relaxes back, lets go. "Eagle doesn't get 'technical.' Oh, he can *be* technical—I've seen him fix some highly random things on his precious skidcycle—but he can never explain *how*. Not when it's right in front of him, and certainly not in whatever secret letters you shared. If you shared any."

I can't move.

"I've seen the feeds," Reggie says, "and despite the obvious artistry of Mother's pet reporter, 'love-struck' isn't the word that springs to mind."

He knows.

No, he *thinks* he knows.

Shivers take over inside and out.

Wren always says that stories, *good* stories, are about the start and stick—start with the truth and stick with it.

Reggie waits.

Truth.

"My sister's in a coma." Low, almost normal. "Our medics couldn't help, so I tried hacking the inter-House feeds because you have biotech that we don't, but it didn't work."

Dad dismantled the inter-range satellites. There's no hacking that.

"But Wren, my sister, has Dad's military clearance. Communication channels are separate from feed networks, and I thought if I could just talk to someone, find the right specialist, they could do *something*."

Truth. I tried. It didn't work.

But that was *that* story.

"I got patched through, finally, but I didn't know where to start. I didn't have the right names or questions and I couldn't tell people who was asking, so I made things up. Said I was a researcher or a reporter or whoever the medics might listen to, except most of the time they didn't. Then one night, I was really tired and said I was doing an anonymous empathy survey on difficult recoveries—and the medic patched me through to Eagle."

I answered one once. An empathy survey. A medic popped her head in and droned out the required request, barely waiting for my response before closing the door. Only to open it again. *I'm sorry, did you say "yes"?*

"Eagle agreed to a survey?" Reggie asks, equal disbelief and horror.

I rub my arms. "In the medicenter, everyone knows how

you should feel. They don't even agree but they're always right. Be strong, brace up, cry yourself sick, accept it. Sometimes it's just nice to talk to someone who has no answer. Who doesn't care what the answers are. No advice, no sympathy, only bored people asking random unrelated questions that you don't have to answer. Eagle mostly didn't."

I can just see him in the medicenter bed, all wrapped up and bandaged, staring at the flipcom and wondering what his favorite bubblepop flavor had to do with anything.

"But I just kept asking, question after question, because I didn't know what else to do and besides, he sounded so—"

Scratched. Inside out and alone.

"So?" Reggie asks.

But that's between me and Eagle.

"So I said I had to go, but then he asked if I'd call back and I said yes."

And I would have.

Truth.

"Then why aren't you all over each other?" Reggie asks. "Not that I don't appreciate the lack of public display, but still."

I breathe in dust mites and wood as the quiet settles.

"It's different, seeing someone. I mean, in letters the words are all there. But face-to-face I didn't know what to say and I think Eagle thought I'd be—"

Strong, unafraid. Emmie.

"—different."

Reggie doesn't move for a long moment. Then he leans forward and plucks the digislate from my hands. Skims through screens, then lays the slate in my lap and activates a holorecord. A 3-D digital world springs to life—high quality with audio and full spectrum colors.

Elona stands, elbows draped over a low stone wall, hair woven back from her face in large braids that gather at her nape. She's laughing, her earrings a dance of silver sparkles. "—course I'm going to win. You haven't seen Charles ride, have you?"

"No, but I've seen Eagle," holo-Reggie says. He leans beside her, outfitted for riding in tall boots and gloves, head bent in concentration over the black sphere in his hands. A holorecorder, from the shape and size.

A disembodied voice calls, "Is that thing on yet?"

"In a minute," Reggie yells back, adding in an undertone, "Though with any luck, he'll break his damn neck."

Elona laughs as Reggie winks and tosses the recorder high into the air. The scene expands. People cluster in a small grassy clearing alongside a river with steep, rocky banks. On either side, steel ramps swoop in impossibly high arcs on beams that look about as supportive as a bug's legs. Skidcycle ramps.

I shake my head. "No. He wouldn't—no."

But there is Eagle, towering over a golden skidcycle, jacket a blaze of silver and orange. His hair is longer, more haloed, and his face isn't scarred.

I've seen pictures, but not ones that move. Here pieces fit and flow with nothing to break them up.

"Good luck, pretty boy," calls Elona, tiny at the scene's edge. "You'll need it."

Eagle smiles. A subtle smile that is sure of everything. Life is a foregone conclusion he has already won.

On the other side of the river, a different rider—this one in bright green with Charles's gelled spikes—swings a leg over a jet black skidcycle and revs the engine. Eagle raises two lazy fingers, salutes the camera, then mounts up.

My heart skips a beat.

He makes it, I *know* he makes it. He walked me to break-fast this morning.

A call sounds, his wheels spin, and my stupid heart skips again.

The skidcycles fly, flashing in smears of color up the ramps and into the air and Eagle—Eagle leaps not only over the hungry rock river, but *Charles*. He nearly crests the tree line, slowed motion so high above the ground his shadow can't keep up. So high Charles's neck cranes to follow.

Then colors blur and wheels reconnect with ramps and

Eagle's cycle skids to a stop.

My fingers skim through the holo to the screen. "How do I replay that? Which button is it?"

"Asa?" It's Eagle's voice, un-tinny and real. His legs appear beside the desk, crouching as he drops, fingertips brushing the floor. The holo-version waves. Eagle freezes.

"Did you find her?" calls Lady Westlet from beyond the room.

I grin into wary eyes that aren't sure of anything anymore. "You're *amazing*."

Eagle's confusion jumps from me to his brother.

Reggie shrugs. "Apparently, you have a fan."

HEART

THE PALE SCROLLWORK ON LORD WESTLET'S office door has a lion hidden in it. And a puff-fish and a heron with its wings spread. I stretch then raise my hand fast because *this* time I'm going to knock.

I've been summoned, and I am here.

My fist finds wood.

"Come in," calls Lord Westlet and I open the door.

Lord Westlet sits on the corner of his desk, one foot hovering above the floor, suit so deep brown it's almost black. "Asa."

A three letter warning.

"Sir."

"We have a visitor." He nods to the right, and there's Emmie.

An older Emmie in a brown shirt and long white vest jacket. Her hair is braided smooth, eye shadow neutral, shimmery fingernails brown instead of red. Around her right wrist, a faint chain sparkles.

I jump forward. "You're here!"

She takes in my wrinkle-free slacks and the ribbon

157

headband the Lady insists on, and says, "Asa."

"Come." Lord Westlet beckons me with a seemingly carefree hand. "I have a question."

Emmie raises her chin, her gaze fixed over my head like I'm not enough of somebody to be real.

She knows about Elona.

"Asa," says Lord Westlet.

Lord Westlet pats the desk beside him, smile no more or less than it was before. I stand where indicated and straighten my shoulders, like Emmie. "The Lady has my word, sir. I will do better."

"Excellent. However, that is not the question."

"My Lord," says Emmie, "if you will—"

"Ah." Lord Westlet raises a tapered finger. "I'm conversing with my daughter."

The daughter I wasn't a few days ago?

Not that I say so or even think it, because I am temperance and tact.

"Now tell me, dear heart, is ecoflux safe? Or do its factories still cause the Blight?"

"No." I raise my head to his bland eyes. "Dad fixed it. He's switched most of the big city power grids over, and the main transits. You can't even buy uleum flightwings anymore."

"So it's safe?"

"Yes."

"So there'd be no reason to retest or reevaluate its schematic?" he asks with casual disinterest, swinging his toe along the floor.

The hairs shift on the back of my neck, and I can feel the vacuum of Emmie's glare. Which makes no sense at all because the answer is yes, it's stable. It's been stable for months.

"Wren was the technician," I say, slow. "She helped build the schematic. I didn't pay that much attention."

"But within your *recent* experience, have you seen any reason to doubt its stability?"

No. The medicenter runs on the new power grid, and while I didn't check the general feeds, Casser would have mentioned if something was that wrong.

I shake my head.

"Ah." Lord Westlet looks past me, flashing teeth. "Tell your father that he has just forfeit the entirety of the first shipment and potentially the second—unless I have those schematics in hand by the end of the week."

"No!" I reach for his sleeve and pull back just in time. "You promised."

His smile transfers to me. "I said once Fane sent the schematics, if you recall. He has not. This, I'm afraid, is beyond your control."

As if anything has ever been in my control.

"Please, you *can't*—"

He waves me away, his words are for Emmie alone. "Do we understand each other?"

The blood disappears from Emmie's face, probably to pool with mine on the floor.

"Perfectly, sir," she says.

"Excellent." Lord Westlet is sleek lines and snake coils. "Now the Lady believes this is an excellent opportunity to impress the newsfeeds. There's a new club in the city she says the young people enjoy, and Eagle will be more than happy to escort you both." The Lord nods at me, without quite glancing over. "Dearest, please go and tell him so. I'll send your sister along shortly."

THE HALL BLURS. LIFE-SIZE PORTRAITS OF PAST WEST-lets catalog my steps, their rich satin and austere smiles line the marbled gray walls.

"He *promised*," I tell their smug faces. "Maybe truth is fluid but your word is not, and *we* would not do that."

Except Dad promised schematics that aren't here.

And an Heir. He promised that, too.

I press my fingertips to the corners of my eyes and gulp hot air from cupped hands.

I have to find Eagle and tell him how happy he is. I can't cry.

I face the whole dead gallery. "I hate you."

And they don't care.

The hall empties to winding stairs that lead to another long passage and finally a windowed sun room with wispy, ruffled curtains. I peer through the lace to the garden beyond.

Eagle stands by the edge of the stone patio, as if his boots ache for grass. Elona perches nearby on a high table-top meant for drinks. Reggie leans against the table, elbow near her thigh, his other hand waving in illustration. The sun sparks off his ring, and skypetals bloom in organized clusters beyond.

On the patio's opposite side, Lady Westlet laughs star-light in a deep purple blouse that billows in the breeze.

Mekenna lounges beside her, face tilted toward the sun, threaded earrings shimmering.

Normal. Everyone fluid, belonging. So sure of their place they don't have to think about it.

Like how we used to look before Dad posted Wren to Urnath, on the nights Emmie didn't have a date and Dad read reports in the living room and Wren spread her dismantled communicator watch over the table and explained what went where and the transmitters that let her issue orders.

Eagle looks toward the window and I jerk away. Press my back to the thin strip of wall between the window and the door. I squeeze too hot eyes, except the burning runs much, much too deep.

Clacked steps. An approaching laugh. "Now, I *would* pay to see that."

Lady Westlet enters, pauses, closes the door. "Asa."

"I'm supposed to get Eagle," I say, mostly steady, "for our itinerary."

"Oh, the club, yes. Lucky your sister flew in today. I'd send Reggie as well, but someone must entertain the cousins." She leans past me to peer out the window. "And he seems quite comfortable as is."

I sidestep to the door. "I'll get Eagle."

"Yes." The Lady rests a hand on my shoulder, drawing

out the word. "Do. In fact, why don't you run up and kiss him?"

"What?"

"Mekenna is a romantic, as much as she tries to bury the fact. She'll never forgive your father for Orrin—and has transferred much of that resentment to *us*—but you? You circumvented an inter-House blood bond to be with a scarred cadet. It's a beautiful day. Your much loved sister is here, whom you've begged to come with you to your concert, and she's agreed. What else would you do, but run out to him in excitement? Not to mention it's your first outing beyond the complex. Yes, I do think you would." She pats my cheek and turns me to the door.

I dig my heels in. "My Lady—"

"Mekenna has come specifically for an update on the husband who had no difficulty forgetting her after two years, when she's been steadfast thirteen. That is not a conversation that bodes well for this House, nor one I can long hedge off. Be a dear and convince her that not all of Fane is evil incarnate." She opens the door and pushes me through.

Everyone looks up.

There's no time.

I run.

"Eagle!" Bright excitement and pure panic.

He turns, barely fast enough to catch me as I lock my

arms around his waist and bury my face in his shirt. His chest presses solid against my every scattered heartbeat.

"Asa?"

The story. Remember the story.

Except his arm curls warmth around my side and his palm curls light around my head, and the only story that matters is the one where he doesn't let go.

"What's wrong?" he asks, and I can feel them. The words. On his lips, in my hair.

"Everything," I whisper.

He shifts, hand skimming feathers down my neck.

"Excuse us," he says, louder now and half distracted, walking us forward. I unwind my arms but his doesn't move, tucked tightly and rippled under his sleeve. His right arm. His left hand opens the door.

Lady Westlet waits.

Eagle nods but doesn't stop. "Mother."

"That was brilliant." She presses the door shut and gently shifts the curtain. "Even better than a kiss. Look at her *face*."

Eagle freezes and my soul cracks.

"Maybe," sighs the Lady, age and exhaustion and hope, "just maybe, we'll pull this off." She rubs Eagle's shoulder and flicks my hair. "Oh, my beautiful children. Well done."

Then she skips from the room.

Slowly, Eagle pulls his arm from my waist. Steps away.

"So you're fine," he says.

I am empty and untethered and not even here.

But that's not the right story. I don't think. My heart is bound in wire and beating blood and I can't remember.

He stares into empty shadows his mother left, lips parted on a word he doesn't say.

Until he does.

"Well done."

"Eagle—" I step forward, reach out.

"What?" Taut as the fists at his sides, he doesn't turn. "Can't we call it done for today?"

My hand drops and I pull it tight behind my back so it doesn't crack with the rest of me. "Yes. Of course."

And he's gone.

THE CLUB LIGHTS TURN EMMIE'S JACKET RED AS IT
swirls around her hips. Glowing wires spiral over the walls
and crisscross the thrumming ceiling. Sound-to-hue translators weave every note into color over endless dancers
who jump and shake and scream. The main act isn't even
on yet.

Emmie flew us in. Eagle used up his rations going to
Malsa, and Emmie's flightwing runs on ecoflux, so she'd
have flown even if he was with us.

Which he isn't.

Someone rams my shoulder. I stumble and my drink
sloshes over the girl ahead, turning her shirt alcohol sticky.

"Hey!" The girl whips around, hair flying. "What the—"

Emmie slides between us. "Stuff it."

The girl huffs away as the band screams and the walls
pulse red.

"If I get you another drink," Emmie half yells, "can you
not douse the natives?"

I shake my head. I don't want a drink. I don't want to be
here; I want Eagle.

Wren. I mean Wren.

Emmie grabs my shoulders, stands on tiptoe to yell in
my ear. "Lady Westlet wants us happy, so be frickin' happy."
She shakes me a little, out of time with the pounding beat.
"Seriously, cheer up."

I shake her off and tug her away from the worst of the crowd, where the colored lights swirl less. Then I round on her. "Why didn't Dad send the schematics?"

He should have, he absolutely should have. He gave his word as Fane.

Her jaw tightens. "Because they're the only hold we have. We need those shipments."

"I *know*. You think I don't know? All I've done is—"

"What? Measure up to the great Lord's standards? You?" She smiles. Nothing hidden, no subtle cut, only truth. The kind that just *is*. She sighs. "Look, I'm sure you're trying, but this is too important to screw up." Her arm snakes around my waist and she squeezes. "Okay?"

Onstage, the music spikes and something stringed dies.

"Come on." She drags me forward, through people pressed arm to arm, back to chest. Legs and bodies and laughter. A stranger's hand brushes my neck, another rubs sweat against my skin, and I can't. I just—

Can't.

I back away from Emmie. The crowd swarms our link. Her bracelet glitters. "Asa, come on."

But if measuring up is impossible, I'll be faithless somewhere else.

I twist free, back up into people who growl but have no problem taking my place. Until Emmie disappears and

I'm alone in the flow, fighting momentum to reach the crowd's edge.

Onstage, the drums explode, pulsing the walls' translators a deep, vibrant red. I shut my eyes and soak them in.

With any luck, they'll swallow me whole.

Another hand settles on my arm and stays there, as if my standing against the wall somehow gave them the right.

"Go *away*." I spin and almost smack into a green jacket. Which slides all the way up into a hood that's too close to hide anything. The color translators bounce light everywhere and reflect in his eyes. Black, brown, and even green on the high notes.

His hand falls.

The drums pound under my skin. "Eagle?"

He says something, a string of somethings, and I don't catch any of it.

"What?" I stand on tiptoe, try to reach his words without leaning in.

But he does. Lean. Palm on my shoulder as my heels sink to the floor, and his lips find my ear, "Mother sent me."

Oh.

I nod. Don't hunch or choke.

Inside, everything chokes.

I point at the crowd, and yell, "Emmie's probably by the stage."

He nods. I wait for him to go after her. Appease the Lady. Dance with the bride he should have had.

"Father's on a tirade," he says, and I swear I feel his lips. "Fane didn't send the schematics?"

He pulls back enough to meet my eyes. Our noses almost touch.

"How mad?" I ask.

"What?" he says. Or rather mouths, for all I can hear him.

I hold the loose edge of his jacket for balance, my cheek brushing his as I stand on tiptoe. "How mad is he?"

Eagle doesn't answer. Or move.

I pull back and tug his jacket, before the panic screams out. "How *mad*?"

Nothing. At all.

I drop his jacket before I scream or bawl or both.

"I have trouble," he says, so close my skin maps all the places we almost touch. "Hearing. On that side. What did you say?"

"What?!" I pull back.

He shrugs, hands finding pockets.

I regrab his jacket and reach up, double-check I'm on his left side, then ask, "Why are you *here*? Doesn't it hurt? Do we need to leave?"

He bends close. "It's fine. What did you say?"

"Really? Because I'll get Emmie and—"

"Positive." Sharp, even over the speakers' wail. "How *what*? What did you say?"

I'm not sure I want to know anymore. "How mad is Lord Westlet?"

"Very. I think he meant to send the initial shipment back with Emmaline. He was yelling over his flipcom to unload the transport."

My legs disappear and I sink.

Eagle catches me before the floor does.

"Steady," he says against my temple. Lips featherlight and reverberating—outflanking the music's rhythm until my heart can't keep time.

But that's the wrong story. A lie, like Dad's promises and everything else.

"Don't." I push away and he stumbles back. "The Lady isn't here, nobody's looking. You don't have to—" But the band screams and the crowd answers and I brush past to find Emmie.

EMMIE WANTS TO EAT, BUT NOTHING'S OPEN. THE whole district is powered down—curved skytowers dark against the rising moon, scattered trees smothering the streetlights.

Emmie stands in the middle of the empty street and glances from the pulsing club a block down, to the high-rise docking bay just ahead. "Lord Westlet sets *curfews*?"

Even at our absolute worst, right before the final eco-flux breakthrough, Dad never set curfews.

He just handed out ration tokens and made people set their own.

Eagle shrugs. "It conserves energy."

"And you're obviously in desperate need of conservation." Emmie waves at the club that Dad wouldn't even bother regulating tokens to.

And maybe the Westlets wouldn't, either, if they weren't trying to stave off the Electorate.

"Let it go, Emmie," I say.

She places her hands on her hips, prepping for the fight she's been burning for all evening. As if the club's pulsing red pumped into her soul.

"Please," I say. Not tonight. "Dad lied about the schematics. Isn't that enough?"

She looks down the street. Over at the darkened tower shop fronts. Back toward the club.

Everywhere but at me.

"Emmie," I say, slow. "Dad *did* lie, didn't he? He didn't send the schematics with you. You don't have them, right?"

"Of course not." Her laugh bounces high, and she cuts it off the next second. "Why would I?"

"Because they're our only real bargaining chip. Because if Lord Westlet has the schematics, you think we'll have no leverage to get the food. Because this is too important and you think I'll screw it up."

Eagle shifts beside me.

"Give them back," I say. "Just give them back, and—"

Emmie's face shuts down and she *becomes* power. Her heel slides back a step. "You're talking nonsense."

"Emmie." I step forward.

She bolts for the docking bay. I make three steps to follow before Eagle snags the back of my shirt.

"There's people. That bay was packed coming in. We'll stop her in the air." His free hand pulls a flipcom from his pocket and snaps it open.

"No!" I swipe it away. "*No.* She's protecting us—Fane—don't you see? She doesn't think I'll measure up, she doesn't think I *can.* And once I fail and your dad has the schematics, then we'll never get the food because we'll have nothing else to offer."

"Then she's an idiot. Give me the com." Eagle reaches

out but I jump back and stumble off the curb.

"You don't understand." I shake my head, still backing up. "Dad will kill her, he won't forgive that. He can't. It'll be Mom all over again."

Especially if Emmie goes home and acts like everything's fine. She's probably already asked Dad to let her handle communications with Westlet—so she can step up, do her part. And Dad would agree because it's the kind of thing Wren would do. Then Emmie will hold the schematics hostage for the food, thinking Lord Westlet will cave first, except he won't. He'll pay back in kind, Dad will find out, and Wren won't be the only one in a coma.

"I will fix this, okay? Give me a week, just a week, and I will *fix* this I swear. Please. Don't tell your dad."

"Okay," says Eagle.

"He'll tell *my* dad, and Dad can't know, not *ever*."

"Okay."

"And I know you don't believe me, but I will make this right I swear."

"I know." And the certainty echoes in his watching frame.

"You know?" I ask.

"She's your sister, Asa. Of course you'll get them."

FAITHLESS

"I 'VE INVITED COUSIN EVIE TO JOIN US TOMORROW," says Elona, midway through breakfast. "I do hope that's all right."

Lord Westlet's knife pauses over the butter, and the Lady's spoon clinks in her bowl.

"From my mother's side, you know." Elona's hair is piled high on her head and bubbles with her voice. "She flew in last night, if you can believe it, and while I hate taking liberties I would so love to spend some quality time with her before she's off again. I hardly ever get to see her anymore." Elona flashes me a small cat smile. "And I think she would love to see the way our little family has grown."

My retribution.

Electorate names speed through my head, but I can't find an Evie. Which isn't surprising because it's next to impossible to pin them all down.

I can't see Eagle. He's lost behind Charles's gelled spikes.

"Of course," says Lord Westlet, slicing the butter. "Always pleased to entertain family."

Elona beams. "Excellent."

I beam right back. Smooth my crinkled napkin into thin, crisp folds under the table.

Maybe Evie lost her family in the lockdown. Maybe her sole goal in life is to see Fane fall. Maybe she knew Eagle.

Maybe he loved her.

Maybe he still does.

Lady Westlet lays down her spoon and lifts her glass. "Asa, dear, how would you like to go shopping?"

SINCE URNATH, EMMIE SAYS I LOOK LIKE A BOY. THIS dress proves her wrong. The lace shimmers silver, balances my skin and shows most of it. As in cleavage. I don't have much, but the dress doesn't seem to care.

I am very pretty in the mirror. Soft edges and static hair that flies every which way without seeming too messy.

I am nothing like Evelyn Tress, who is strength and energy and looked like she could jump off the screen—the digislate was too small to hold her. Elona has several cousins, and several more who might be cousins, including at least three Evie's.

But only one is training for the Special Guard.

"No, no, absolutely not." Lady Westlet walks around me as I stand before the curved fitting room mirror. "I said elegance and *power*, Martina. These sleeves are puffed."

Evelyn Tress is nothing but power. In one of the news articles, she was leaning against a skidcycle.

"Yes, but it suits her, my Lady," Martina nearly whines, a mere shell of the regal matron who greeted us when we entered her boutique.

Four hours and thirty-two dresses ago.

She waves at me, her hair now almost as wispy as mine. "My lady Asa simply hasn't the figure for—"

Lady Westlet finds Martina's eyes in the mirror.

"Yes?" purrs the Lady. "Pray continue."

Martina doesn't, cheeks pale as her blonde bun.

"For *that*," I finish. I wave at the far wall, with its floor-to-ceiling embedded screens featuring beautiful models in beautiful clothes who twist for inspection. "I'm not elegance or power and she can't create what isn't *here*."

The closest wall-screen model raises a slender, seductive arm and says, "*Regal Reflections* by Desvoni, because you are the core the world reflects."

The Lady *is* a regal reflection. "Martina, might we have a moment?"

"Of course, my Lady." Martina bows low and makes good her escape.

The Lady doesn't move or speak, rosewater perfume softening the boutique's over-rich musk.

I kick at the floor, what little isn't covered in discarded shoes and head scarves. "It's not her fault."

Lady Westlet doesn't sag, I doubt she's even capable, but all the threads holding her up dissolve into nothing. "I know. I can only imagine how difficult this must be." She shakes her head as if to shed her thoughts. "We do not get to choose what we face, only how we face it. You have done well, Asa, and you will do this."

I DON'T KNOW THE STARS. THEY TANGLE BLUE WHITE in the black, and I can't name any of them. I hug my knees, my sleep clothes no match for the wind. Beyond the balcony, the tiered shadows of the House block out the woods. Windows dark, everyone asleep. Or pretending to be.

I'll ask to go home. Say I need to get Wren's scans for a new medichip. Which means throwing away the ones I have and the vials in case they search. I'll just get more. Lord Westlet will think I'm worried for Wren and let me go, and once home I'll access the End-Level network and get the schematics. Wren gave me access during quarantine so I could dig for the files and scans she needed instead of her. It should still be active unless Dad found out and revoked it. He never said he revoked it.

But then, he wouldn't.

Someone screams.

I flatten against the wall. Another cry—muffled and piercing. What Eagle would sound like if he raised his voice.

I'm on my feet and through the glass doors. Long shadows huddle, but nothing moves.

"Eagle?" He's not on the couch or in the chairs, and his door is shut tight. Normal, just like when I went outside. I probably dreamed it. I'm probably just tired and—

He screams again.

It's coming from his room.

I yank his door open and snap on the lights. Eagle, in bed. Murmuring low, slippery things, blankets sliding to the floor as his body rocks in some invisible tide. The ridges of his face flow down his right side and arm, to the stump where his hand should be and isn't.

"It's okay, wake up." I reach for his shoulder, except the skin ripples slick under my palm and maybe it's sore or tender or something and I don't want to hurt him. "It's a dream, I swear it's a dream." I climb onto the bed, press on his unscathed shoulder and chest until he lies still because if he shakes any more he'll fly apart. He might anyway, his skin is that hot.

"Eagle. *Eagle.*"

His eyes snap open.

"It's all right," I say. "It's—"

The bed explodes, the world flips, my back hits the mattress, and Eagle blocks out the ceiling. He leans on his good arm, palm near my head, while the ball of the other presses my shoulder flat.

Unfocused eyes, staccato breath.

I lie very, very still. "Wake up, Eagle."

My lungs burn with his rhythm. I make them slow down.

"It's just me. You can wake up."

He blinks and his eyes aren't so black anymore. They look and look and finally *see*.

I relax into nothing. "Hey."

His gaze skips like maybe I'm real or maybe I'm not—from my face to shirt to shoulder, and freezing where his arm pins me down. But he's not pressing hard, just a warm knot that says he's there. The sheets are warm, too, though not near as warm as the weight of his leg which half covers mine. All the way up my thigh.

Eagle's knee is bent, but his heel still brushes the skin of my ankle because my sleep pants were once Wren's and are too short, even when they weren't threadbare, which they are now and have been for months, and I should really probably get rid of them, though maybe not this particular second.

His chest is skin and scars and muscles and brushes mine on his inhales or exhales or some other breath-related thing he shouldn't be able to do because the oxygen is gone.

His eyes find me staring and I say the only thing in my head that doesn't involve him. "Happy books."

If Eagle thought I was a dream or crazy before, I'm officially both now. His arm presses harder as his balance shifts, bearing too much of his weight, and I slide up and a little away to compensate.

"That's what I do. I have these audiostories on my dig-islate that are funny and when the dreams come, especially the really bad ones, I turn them on and—"

He disappears. Evaporates.

I rise on my elbows.

He sits on the edge of the bed, the left edge, as far from me as possible, all the smooth skin facing me, his handless arm lost in the dark. "Are you all right?"

"Why wouldn't I be?"

"Why are you here?"

"I heard—you were dreaming."

"Well, I'm awake now." Even, controlled. "Go to bed."

I scramble upright. "But do you have a book? I can get you a book; I can even read one to you."

"I'm fine, Asa."

"But Eagle—"

"Just. Get. Out," he says to the floor, left hand bunched in the sheets.

Oh. Right. Evie's coming tomorrow, and I'm confusing stories.

I slip off the bed. My socked feet siren loud as I reach the door. "Sleep well, okay?"

Eagle's back tenses until the scars mold his skin. It's hard to look at him, hard to be within three steps of touching. Hardest of all to close the door with him on the other side.

But I do.

I SCRUB MY FACE WITH HOT WATER, THEN COLD. IN the mirror, my puffy eyes chatter about tears, tears, and more tears like it's something everyone wants to know.

I don't know where Eagle is. The elevator pinged not long after I left his room, and it hasn't pinged since.

I pull on the new dress Lady Westlet finally chose—a sleeveless, understated mix of silver and white—and slip into the living room and wait. Avoid the couch so I don't wrinkle the dress. Knock on his door, just to make sure. I even open it, but the bed's empty.

Eagle is never late. He's always where he should be.

Which means he's already there.

I yank the door shut, and the hard wood stings. It's *wrong*. Maybe I'm not Cousin Evie and maybe I'm mixing up stories, but we're the treaty, *us*, and I shouldn't have to go in there alone.

I rest my forehead against the door and I wait. And wait.

The elevator doesn't ping.

And it's too late to wait anymore.

BREAKFAST IS A RETICENCE OF GHOSTS. THE CLOUDY gray window light dulls everyone's smiles and clothes. Even the plates and knives are quiet.

I scan the heads. Lord and Lady Westlet, Reggie and the cousins, a man in a deep purple suit, and a woman too old to be Evelyn.

Eagle didn't come without me.

He didn't come at all.

"There she is," Elona calls from near the end of the table, resplendent in silver and purple and very adult. "We'd quite given you up."

I hurry toward an empty chair. "I'm so sorry! Eagle"—isn't here, why isn't he here?—"couldn't sleep, so I found him some pills, except I think they were too strong because I couldn't get him up." The Lady shoots me a look, and I add, "He's fine, I wouldn't have come if he wasn't, but I am sorry."

"Don't be," says the woman seated across the table, one place down from the chair I stand behind. She stands, too, and even in the clouded sunshine, her bodice and skirt sparkle purple stardust. She's like the Lady in height and age but softer-jawed and springy as her slightly frizzy hair. Blonde hair, oddly familiar, loose and escaping its pins. "My dear, dear child. How you have grown."

Grown?

I can't get the word to make sense, it won't translate. Or maybe it's the voice. Something about the voice.

Everyone watches like we're at a dance.

The space beside me is very, very Eagle-less.

She smiles, wide and warm, like we share a secret.

I used to sneak into Wren's room when I was little and play with the mini techbots she built for class. That's how I found the holorecord of the woman in the glitter dress—with her luminescent eyes and swishy skirt. She'd chatter endlessly about a concert or a party or something, but her dress was perfect and starry and I didn't even notice when Wren came in.

She yanked the digislate from my hands. *You tell Dad, you're dead, do you hear me? Dead.*

I scooted back against the wall, because when Wren got really *really* mad, she could be scary. But all she did was hug the slate and look at me. Just looked. *You don't remember, do you?*

"You remember me, don't you?" asks the woman who isn't Evie or Evelyn.

Not that Dad ever says her name.

But it's not her, it can't be. She's too pretty—prettier than the holorecord, mouth quirking like Emmie's does when she laughs, long legs peeking out from the swish of her skirt.

She always wore skirts. Fluttering, pretty things I'd

tumble after on too-short legs, trying to catch them like but-
terflies. They sparkled so, but tasted gritty.

I can still feel them, the flaky sticky bits, acrid on
my tongue.

"You *do* remember," says the woman who can't be here
because the Westlets wouldn't let her in. Wouldn't sit with
her and smile over coffee like it's nothing. Like she has
every right to be here. Like she didn't sell us out to Galton
and nearly break our House.

But she is here, prancing around the table, bony arms
stretching from embroidered sleeves. "Oh, sweetheart, I've
missed you."

Missed me? She doesn't *know* me.

She left when I was three.

"Genevieve." Glitter and grit.

"So formal." She seeps into the space where Eagle isn't.
"We can begin better than that."

She holds out her arms.

Lord Westlet throws a too-languid elbow over his
chair's back while resignation shines from under the Lady's
half-closed lids.

They're already calculating the fallout. My inability to
measure up.

I don't have any smiles in me, not even fake ones,
but my tongue still works. "Mother." I step forward and let

her arms snake around my waist. I pat a back so thin I feel her spine.

When I pull away, she keeps an arm around me.

Down the table, Elona meets my eyes and raises her glass in a toast.

Stay still. Just. Stay. Still.

"My baby." Genevieve lays her head on my shoulder because that's all she comes up to. "I was so worried. Gavin can be such a grudge holder, I hate to even *think* what he told you. Nothing worth repeating, I'm sure."

No, Dad said nothing. Absolutely nothing.

Except to tell me I was hers.

"But there now, you're here and out of that cursed lockdown." She pulls me toward the suited stranger, who is already rising to his feet. He's familiar somehow, round faced and light skinned, with short ashy brown hair. His purple cuffs are etched with the same threaded blue as Genevieve's dress.

Galton colors.

Genevieve rubs the shoulder of what must be Dad's replacement. He smiles from a height that matches mine and measures me by inches.

I might be up for sale.

"A pleasure to meet you, *my* girl." He holds out his hand at the odd emphatic *my*.

Timing is everything in a handshake, and I count the seconds.

One, two, three.

Four.

"You as well," I say, taking his too-smooth, too-hot palm.

"Asa!" Genevieve chides. "Doesn't your father get a hug, too?"

I freeze.

So does everyone else. We're in a holorecord with no Pause button. Even Elona's smugness has gone.

You have done well, Asa, and you will do this.

I take back my hand, slow and steady, so the words come slow and steady, too. "My father is in Fane. But if he was here, I'm sure he'd also be pleased to meet you."

"Gavin?" Genevieve laughs. "I very much doubt it."

"A deeply moving reunion," says Lord Westlet, his voice airy razored silk. "Really, the heart bleeds. But perhaps, my Lady, it might continue after breakfast?"

He doesn't linger on the title but it is definitely there, the *Lady*, with the full House weight.

But Genevieve lost that title when she lost Dad. The Triplicate holds only Lady Westlet and Lady Galton, and Genevieve can't be Lady Galton because she's *old*. Lady Galton's Heir is a son around Dad's age. Even with lockdown, Dad would have said if a House Lady died, even

Galton's. If he had known, he would have *said*.

Wouldn't he?

But this man is Dad's age and so very familiar.

"Yes, of course, forgive me." Genevieve's nod is everything gracious, hair slipping into the Wren-blue eyes. "Gavin has kept you trapped for much too long, but he hasn't a right and we will prove it. We won't let him steal you again, will we Jaered?"

"No." The man kisses her reaching fingers. "We hold on to our own."

Then he smiles.

A round-cheeked, uneven Asa smile.

His nose is bigger than mine, but turns up at the tip the same way. He has my hair, and the eyebrows that don't quite match. The pale, uninteresting lips that Emmie says I should always bury in color.

Me in a way Dad never was.

A ringing kicks up in my head, creeping high and higher, until it drowns *everything*. Lord Westlet stands in slow motion. The Lady, too, then everyone. A mimed disharmony of mouths and feet, all focused on the man who is me and isn't and can't be.

I step back. Once. Twice.

And I'm gone.

DAUGHTER

"DAD!" I SAY INTO LORD WESTLET'S FLIPCOM. I'm in the Lord's office, under his desk. It took forever to connect through the one open channel, even with Lord Westlet's communications ID.

"Asa?" And it's him, really him.

"You have to tell them. You have to tell them I'm not his."

"What?"

"She says they're going to steal me back because you have no right and, Dad, he looks like me—like *me*—and you have to tell them I'm yours, because whatever I say they'll keep talking but they won't with you, you can prove it. Please, you have to come."

His voice drops. "She?"

"Genevieve. She was at breakfast, Dad. *Breakfast.* And they're calling her Lady and this Jaered is with her and—"

"Galton's there?"

"No, Dad, *listen.* Not Lady Galton, but Genevieve and this Jaered person—"

"Jaered is Galton. His mother died two years ago."

Galton? *Lord* Galton? My mom is *Lady*—?

My palm buzzes with their polite, treacherous hand-shakes, and I scrape it against the carpet.

"How long have you known?" I ask, but Dad's already moved on.

"What did your mother say?"

It doesn't matter what she said, it's what he *didn't*. "Did you know she was related to the Electorate?"

"Distantly, what—"

"Did you know she was a cousin?"

"Fourth or fifth, what—"

"Why didn't you tell me?"

"I told Emmaline." Ragged and echoing.

Right, of course. This is her role, her place. She doesn't look like *him*.

"What did your mother say, Asa? What exactly?"

"That you're not my dad."

"And that Galton was?"

I nod, which is stupid. "Yes."

Maybe he nods, too, because he doesn't answer.

He won't come. He didn't for Wren. He won't for me.

Not if it means seeing Genevieve.

"I should go," I say.

"Asa."

"It's okay, Dad." It's not, but it's not like he'll be here

to care. "Even if no one listens, I can get a blood signature or something to prove—"

"No." Immediate and harsh. "I will be there tomorrow. Do not give them the idea if they haven't had it yet. Don't say *anything*."

"Dad?"

"Though knowing your mother, I'm sure they have. Do *not* let her near you."

"But I'm yours, it won't matter if—"

"Blood bonds require actual blood, but she's resourceful. Don't give her the opportunity."

"But Dad, I'm—"

"*Asa.*" Three letters strung by thread. "I will handle this."

The flipcom slips to the floor as I lift my hands. *Dad's* hands. Wren said so. When we used to play Slap Spades, Emmie would whine because we were faster, and Wren would press my palm to hers, spread all the fingers out and say, *That's because we have Dad's hands and you don't, so there.*

"NICE TRY." REGGIE PEERS UNDER THE DESK, ANGER pulsing in his temple, backlit by the light he has switched on. "But this is *your* mess, and you'll face it with the rest of us."

He grabs my arm and hauls me to the elevator and up four flights. There's rhythm in the marching. I count our steps, the passing doorknobs, the wall sconces.

But all I hear is Dad.

Reggie yanks open the door to the small library and pushes me through. "The Daughter of Fane, as requested."

The storytelling windows warm everything but Lord Westlet. He paces thunder while the Lady watches from an armchair and rubs her temples.

I stand in the middle of the room, assessed and alone.

From behind, Reggie says, "Or should I say, *Galton*?"

"No," I say, but it holds no depth or weight. Not enough to stay upright.

Except Lord Westlet catches my arm and pushes me into the chair by the Lady. "Get out."

I try to rise, but the Lady rests two fingers on my hand and keeps me in place.

"*Now*, Reggie," says Lord Westlet.

Reggie slams the door. The Lord picks up his battle march.

Thirty-four steps. Thirty-eight. Forty-six.

"NO, I WILL *NOT* CALM DOWN! THE STABILITY OF OUR House rests on a Daughter of Fane who—besides not being the Heir—isn't actually *Fane*."

"We don't know that, Arron."

"You saw them! You saw them both!"

"Just because there's a slight similarity—"

"*We have her mother's word.* And if Genevieve is *sure*, I'm sure Fane has at least *guessed*—an interesting little tidbit he failed to mention."

"The arrangement was for Emmaline—"

"No, the arrangement was for the damn *Heir*, not that it matters now, because if the girl is Galton's, then her *blood* is Galton's, and our treaty is *with* Galton—*and*, might I point out, we don't even have Fane's damn energy schematics! Should Galton decide to strip our planets as bare as the independents, we won't have the power enough to stop him without stripping our planets *ourselves*, and won't the Electorate love that? 'Oh, by the way, I've decided to annihilate your home world, would you mind moving out?'"

"I'm sure Fane will deliver—"

"*But* if we hold fast to our son's lying bastard of a father-in-law, we will be in direct violation of the treaty—since we are blood bonded through *Galton's Daughter*, and the Electorate will back his right!"

"We've no proof she's—"

"And should we fail to honor *that*, Daric could oust our line! Or prep a militia for the attempt, which he has been quietly building over on Olev—don't think I don't know—and waste the last of our energy on a civil war that neither of us have a hope of winning. *Especially*, if Mekenna withdraws her support. She has been our one steadfast ally, and now we may not even have *her*."

"Yes, but we don't know for certain Asa is—"

"Not to mention that without Fane's fuel—or, God forbid, the man himself—our whole House will go dark. We'll be sent back to the damn preflight age, though at least they had separate energies for light and heat and flight. Not that they could fly, but at least their entire power structure *wasn't* uleum based."

"Arron."

"Where the hell is Eagle?"

"Asa, dear, where *is* Eagle?" Lady Westlet looks at me. They both do, with the Lord pausing on step eighty-six.

"On his skidcycle," I say, which feels true even if it's wrong. I don't think he has fuel rations enough.

Lady Westlet sinks back into her chair. "You quarreled."

"What?" The Lord throws up his hands. "Quarreled? *Our* little lovebirds? Impossible!"

"Arron," the Lady says with a sigh.

"They are the love story of the century, they couldn't

possibly *quarrel*. She drugged her sister so they could live happily ever after. A sister who, no doubt, is *full-blooded Fane*." He rounds on me, the lines near his mouth etched deep. "Did you know? Did you?"

I press into the chair so hard it presses back. "I have Dad's hands."

He tips his head to the ceiling, "God forgive my misconception. She has her father's hands."

"*That is enough.*" The Lady rises in a whirlwind of arms and skirts. "The girl obviously had no idea, and if you bothered looking at her face instead of screaming into it, you wouldn't need to ask."

"They'll petition for her blood signature, you know that."

"No," I say. "No tests. Dad said."

Their stares scrape bone.

"Forgive me," says Lord Westlet, "but *when* did he say?"

"I called him from your office," I tell the carpet. "The border techs patched me through. He said he'd handle it."

"That was his entire comment? He'd *handle* it?" He presses splayed fingers to both temples. "Still think she's Fane?"

"*Yes.*" I bound from the chair, place my palm flat against my chest. "I don't care what you or Genevieve or anybody else says, because I know who I am. I *know*."

The Westlets share a glance, an entire conversation.

"Oh, Asa," says the Lady. Not a contradiction or agreement or even hope—just, "Asa."

LORD GALTON'S FACE FILLS EAGLE'S DIGISLATE. I HOLD it up beside my head in the bathroom mirror. A close-up wasn't as hard to find as I expected. Amazing how accessible everything is when your House isn't in lockdown.

He doesn't have my forehead. His eyes are lighter, jaw stronger, neck wider. We're less alike in pictures. If my hair wasn't so short, I wouldn't have noticed a resemblance. Not unless I was looking. I might have noticed in a holorecord.

Dad probably has a holorecord.

My bedroom door thumps, but it's locked tight. Genevieve will have to break it down to get in.

Maybe I should push the bed in front of it.

More thumps.

"Go away," I yell. If she wants temperance, she can go pound on Lady Westlet's door.

"It's me." Brusk and entirely Eagle. "Just me."

I reinvent speed—cross the room, deactivate the lock, and throw open the door. *"Why?"*

Eagle looks like he hasn't slept since yesterday. Or the year before. Jacket dusty, boots encrusted in mud.

As if that's an excuse. I step back into my room and slam the door.

Or try to. He catches it.

"Go away," I say, "or better yet, *get out*."

He winces. "I heard. What happened."

"I'm sure you did." I push and push, but his arm's solid rock. "I'm sure everyone in the whole universe knows by now."

His shoulders wedge between the frame and there's no point pushing anything. I fling the door wide. Eagle stumbles, but keeps his feet instead of falling over.

"*I waited for you.*" Harsh as Dad, my dad, my *real* dad.

Eagle goes still.

"I waited and waited and then I went to breakfast, by myself, *alone.*"

His eyes close and seconds burn. "I'm sorry."

"And that makes it better?"

"No." Unhesitant, eyes open. "No."

I hug my arms. "Why didn't you tell me who Cousin Evie was? Who she was *married* to?"

"Mother said to leave it. That you were upset and I shouldn't make it worse."

"Did I say leave it? Me? *She* doesn't get to decide! Not her or Genevieve or even Dad, I don't care. You don't get to tell me who I am or who my people are because I know who they are and they're *mine*. I have *people.*"

"Yes. You do." Like it was never in doubt. He takes a step. "Asa—"

"Where were you?"

"The south flats. I ran out of uleum."

So he did take his skidcycle.

"If you weren't going to breakfast, you should have *said*."

"I meant to be back. I didn't check the gauge." His hands dig deep into his pockets. "I scared you."

"Scared me? You weren't even there!"

"Last night." Tense as his taut arms. "I'm sorry."

I rub my chest, the tight charred mess of it. "I wasn't scared."

"Yes, you were. You were talking like you do when—"

"Eagle." If one more person tells me who I am and how I feel, I will raze the world in screams. "I wasn't *scared*."

Shadows swallow his parted lips, but he doesn't argue. Only holds out his hand. "You trust me?"

"To tell me what's going on?"

"To get you out," he says, palm catching the dim light. "The Galtons want your signature. Tomorrow. They've already asked Mekenna for her lab and told half the Electorate you're their blood."

My heart slips out of beat.

I clasp his hand. "They can't. Dad said I can't be tested."

"I know." Eagle steps so close his boots almost brush my toes. "Until Galton can prove it, the blood bond holds. *We* hold. With Fane. So we disappear."

"What?" I pull back, search his face, but he's serious. "Where?"

"The independents."

"But there are none left! Galton—"

"Didn't get them all. There are a few."

But that's not right, because Dad didn't say any had survived. Just like he didn't say Galton had a new Lord.

"For how long?" I ask. "When do we come back?"

Eagle looks at his feet. Or maybe at our clasped hands.

Oh.

The treaty holds as long as I'm not tested. We don't come back.

I don't come back.

"Okay." I slide my hand away. "Okay. I'll have to take your flightwing, but I'm sure your dad will—"

"I'm coming with you," he says, as if I missed that part.

I shake my head. "If I can't be tested, then that's forever. *Forever*, forever, Eagle. You didn't break anything, your blood is fine. You'll stay with your home and family, and I'll—"

"*We're* forever." He resnatches my hand, weaves our fingers. "That's how this works. If you can lose Wren, I can lose Reggie. Trust me. Now pack up, we need to be gone in an hour."

FUEL

MIRROR GIRL IS WHITE BLONDE. I'M NOT SURE I like her. She looks too much like the woman at the breakfast table. The bathroom lights of Eagle's flightwing drain her color away until she's a sea-ghost. At least she's a ghost who doesn't look like Asa.

That's something.

I reach under the counter's edge and tip the fold-out vanity back into the wall. The room is a cross between a shower stall and a jewel box, and unless all the pull-outs are tucked away, the door won't open. Outside, the main room isn't much bigger. It's currently a kitchen, with a yellow countertop and stacked food heater. But with those folded back, the room could be an office or a bed-room. There's likely a fold-down bed somewhere. Probably just one.

With legs and sheets and Eagle.

He sits at the yellow fold-down table, one hand spin-ning through a 3-D holomap. The other rests on the table-top, biotech fingers twitching as he spreads them out and curls them in. Open, closed. Open.

He said we're forever.

Of course we're forever, we're the treaty. That's what he meant.

I think that's what he meant.

"Do you know Evelyn Tress?" I ask.

He looks up, map freezing as he fixates on my head. The whole blonde mess of it. "Elona's cousin? Why?"

"Is she nice?"

"Not particularly," he says, almost a question. "Reggie likes her."

"Oh. Good." I sink into the chair opposite his.

Eagle shakes out his fingers. Asks a slow, "Why?"

"I thought she was Elona's Evie. She came up on the feeds." I nod at his hand. "Does it hurt?"

"It's fine." He restarts the holomap. Tiny planets float over the table in a three-color overlay. Brown, silver, purple. Fane, Westlet, Galton.

Fane arcs in a half-moon along the edge closest to Eagle, the smallest of the three with two systems and twenty-six planets.

Next, Westlet weaves around us over a much greater expanse. Fifty-eight planets. Beyond, larger than us both combined, Galton eats everything. One hundred nine planets covering most of the table.

"The uleum stations in SPAZ distance are here, here,

and here." Eagle's finger moves between two Westlet planets and one from Fane. "Or here, in Galton. We'll need three full recharges to make the closest independent. Or five for Erris, which is safer."

"Do we have five recharges?" Eagle took Reggie's rations before we left, but still. Five.

He shakes his head. "One."

"If we leave through home, we could get an ecoflux wing."

His left thumb rubs circles along his jumpy right palm. "We couldn't refuel outside of Fane, and someone would tag the wing. If your dad covers for us, the Electorate will call him on it."

I reach through the map for Eagle's biotech hand and pull it back across the table. Twist it thumb side down, and feel along the outer edge for the operations panel. Wren said our biotechnology is based on Westlet ideas—they developed it first—so Eagle's hand shouldn't be too different from Casser's.

Eagle goes absolutely still. "What are you doing?"

"It's jammed." The panel controls are below the thumb instead of the wrist, but work the same way. His palm membrane protector fades from skin to circuits. Fat, disorganized circuits, shinier than Casser's but apparently just as faulty.

"You need an upgrade." I poke through jammed connectors, straighten the dislodged bits. Leave the overstrange, complicated pieces alone. "This is old, older than Casser's. I know Westlet has better tech than this."

"Won't work with my chip."

"Your medichip?" The circuits look happy. I reactivate the skin membrane. Slide his hand back. "Why would that matter?"

"It just does." He slowly bends his fingers—one, two, all of them—in and out, fast and faster. They don't glitch.

"What about your ear?" I ask. "Is it hurting? Can you hear at all? You know, at Wren's medicenter there's a specialist who—"

He reaches out, hand blanketing mine on the table, and looks. Just looks. Until my chest heaves at the weight of it.

"I think you should go home," I say.

"No." He lets go and zooms the map on the closest corner of Westlet. "There's a ration base in the left quadrant. It's dry, but Father keeps emergency backups. My print will get us through security, but they'll know we're there. We'll have to be fast. In and out."

Casser kept emergency backups, too. Fourteen full tanks in case something happened to him and Wren "went off the deep end trying to fix it." He never told her they existed. He never told anyone except me, and me only because Wren needed something from the sublevel datarecord storage and I stumbled upon him checking the stock.

"What?" asks Eagle.

The base fell, but even if people invaded the sublevels, they couldn't access the tanks—the palm-print security lock tied only to Wren and Casser. And me with Wren's security bypass, which requires my print to work. It's safe now, the whole planet's been dusted. Fully decontaminated and forever, irrevocably dead.

"Asa?"

Dad would know once we crossed the Fane border, but not where we went. And if we left fast enough, he wouldn't be able to stop us. He could even use that to prove we weren't in-House, if the Electorate asked where we were. If they even knew we crossed the border in the first place.

Eagle's fingers find mine. "Asa?"

"I can get us fuel."

NO ONE HAILS US IN URNATH SPACE. NO FLIGHT coordinators ask for identity codes or destinations. The planet fills the viewshield, bold and bright amid white rings like nothing's changed. We enter the atmosphere. Lower through berry-blue sky and fluff-candy clouds into—

My eyes slam shut and stay shut as the flightwing dips and slows. Until motion stops, the engine dies, and my chest splits.

Wake up. Wren's hand on my shoulder, leaning down. *We're here.*

Except the fingers are too long to be Wren's.

You might as well open your eyes. I know you're awake.

Shadows curl along a public docking bay enclosed in pavement and grime, peppered with the abandoned husks of flightwings. Dead and broken.

Wren couldn't rebuild what the riots busted, but she always tried to keep the streets clean.

"Is it as bad outside?"

"Worse."

THE CITY USED TO SING. BEAUTIFUL OR ANGRY, HAPPY or scared, it always sang. Now it doesn't even breathe.

Towers crowd the sky in bony steel. The half-eaten thoroughfare stretches through a clutter of trash and street-hovers and buildings that didn't survive the bombs. Cracks trickle underfoot, as if our steps break the street.

One skytower rises over the others, dripping casing and wire. Remnants of white glossy steel peek through the rust. High walkways gape to nowhere.

I stop and Eagle does, too.

"That's it," I say. "Central Rise. The base entrance."

He cranes his head back, taking it in. "The tanks are here?"

There's something left? he doesn't add.

"The emergency supplies are underground," I say.

Climbing through the tower's front window requires two hands. Even reinforced rivenglass can't withstand a flightwing's full-speed assault, and a wing's blackened tail still protrudes from the building. I scramble up its creaking body, scrape through rust and grit to duck under the jagged glass. My foot catches on a ridge and the world tilts before Eagle clamps me back against his chest.

"Careful."

Nothing about the main lobby of Central Rise is careful. The whole space is encapsulated in shredded tile and bloody smears. The once-white walls stand guard over pockets of crumpled bones. Clothed, corroded, snapped in odd angles. People bones.

So many. So very many.

We're the only standing, living things in this entire broken world.

"They didn't claim the bodies?" Eagle asks.

I shake my head and it's hard, almost impossible to stop. "We had to get people out. Everything was contaminated and crazy and we didn't have enough soldiers. It was more important to help the living."

Than to bury the dead.

"We should get moving." Harsh and tight.

I nod.

Ghosts whisper across the floor as we climb down the charred wing.

EAGLE'S PENLIGHT PAINTS RIBBONS IN THE DARK. Room after room, stair after stair, face after decayed face. The bodies stop on sublevel 3.

Emergency supplies are on sublevel 22.

Twenty-two's hall ends like the others, smooth except for the embedded screen that glows bright as always. Eagle wipes off its dust with his sleeve. "There's power?"

"It's on a mini renewable solar-circuit." I flatten my hand on the screen. It scans my print and blinks twice. Before the final *access denied* blink, I tap the override key-pad and plug in Wren's code. *Denied* switches to *granted*, and the wall slides away.

Overhead fluorescents pop on, one after the other—a sequenced linear rhythm that blinds after so much dark. I squint until the glare fades into white walls and tile and long metal shelves.

Open crates lay sideways over tumbled boxes and scattered packing foam. Tiny digislate identity tags hang off shelves and lie busted on the floor. Everything raided and consumed.

"God," whispers Eagle.

I walk through the parallel, picked-over shelves. Count them off. At the twenty-third row I turn right, into datarecord storage. The shelves are untouched here, stacked with neatly packed boxes. Historical backups, nonsensitive and unimportant. Nothing anyone would bother with. I drop to my knees at the third shelf from the end, beside the massive crates housed on the lowest rack.

When I grab the closest crate's handle, Eagle takes the other side and the crate slides to the floor. I pop the latch.

Neat, even rows of datarecord circuit boards.

I slide my fingers under the middle one. It lifts out along with the whole false circuit-covered top.

Below lie three neatly packed metal canisters labeled ULEUM.

"See?" I say. "Told you."

We have to carry them up.

Fourteen canisters up twenty-two levels. Eagle digs out some packing cord, makes a harness, and carries two. I barely manage one. We make two trips, six canisters total. Climb and descend, climb and descend.

And the dead watch.

EAGLE CROUCHES BEFORE THE CANISTERS LINED along his wing's hull and scans their labels with his digi-slate. Grease smears his forehead, and his pants are grimy. I soak in the afternoon sun, hug a coffee mug between aching fingers. My second cup.

During quarantine, this would have been my sixth cup. Or my eighth. Casser would be blaring down the people-packed street that everyone *would* get fed today if they waited their turn. I'd be running circles in the main distribution tent, lining up ration packets and telling the soldiers which of the waiting families were due for what—a job Casser wasn't thrilled with me having, but Wren over-rode him. Everyone knew me. We were telling a story, and I was the next best thing to her or Dad. People needed to see a Daughter working on ground level. It showed solidarity. Gave hope.

You're evil! The girl had cried when her turn came, gaunt cheeks and stick arms. *You think you're better, but you're not. You're just evil and I hate you and I hope you die.*

"Asa?"

I jump. Coffee sloshes lukewarm waves over my dirt-black fingers.

"Do you know if—" Eagle stops when I face him.

I glance down, but my shirt is so caked in grit, splashed coffee shouldn't matter. "Yeah?"

The digislate disappears as he stands. "It's late."

It's not really, not according to Urnath's sun, but we weren't under Urnath's sun when we woke up this morning. Or yesterday. Sometime. I can't remember.

"Shouldn't we get the other tanks?" I ask.

"Tomorrow," he says.

EAGLE'S FEET HANG OFF THE MATTRESS. THE BED IS as small as the room and we have to tuck tight against the cold walls to keep our shoulders from touching. We're both on our backs. Maybe that's normal for him, but not for me. Turning away feels wrong and facing him is too something, but there's nowhere to move and I almost wish he was in the cockpit because then my limbs could just be tired and not so very *aware*. Limbs and shower soap. Sheets and skin.

He should be home in a bed that fits. Not in a ghost city on a ghost planet, with a ghost girl who isn't anyone's anymore.

"I think you should go home," I say. "No one's looking for you."

"No."

"Eagle."

"*No.*" One word shouldn't be able to fill so much space.

Exhaustion sticks to my lashes, but there's too much dark and too much him.

"Did you have to walk far?" I ask. "When you ran out of fuel?"

He shifts, shrugs maybe. "Been practicing."

With me, every day, twice a day, for an hour.

"At least we won't have to walk anymore."

A hesitant, "Yeah."

I look over, but the dim blue safety light from the

cockpit illuminates exactly nothing. "You hate walking."

"No, I don't."

"You never talk."

"You do."

A weird gumminess sinks deep in my chest and spreads. "You . . . ?"

He can't like me talking. Nobody likes me talking. Even Wren liked me best quiet.

"What?" Eagle asks.

But if he means something else and the gumminess frosts over, I'll shatter in half.

"You think we'll make it?"

A movement. A touch. Fingertips on the back of my hand. Rough, scraped fingertips sliding across my canister scratches to find my palm. Or my heart, which now beats in the core of my hand.

"Yes."

A whole universe of certainty in a steady voice that can't be sure of anything.

I choke back a laugh. Or a sob, I can't tell. He squeezes my hand and my fingers close tight. Our breath falls into rhythm. We could almost be walking.

"Reggie said I took an emotional survey," says Eagle. "That's how we met."

"I know. I had to say something, so that's what I said."

"What did you ask?"

"Reggie?"

"In the survey."

I shrug against the sheets. "Odd things. They start out normal—how long you've been in the ward, if you like your medics—"

"Six months. Not particularly."

My lungs trip out of sync.

Answers. Actual *answers*.

What did you ask?

If it was real, if I'd called and the medic patched me through, I'd have asked, "Do you have family?"

"Yes."

"Do they visit?"

"Sometimes."

"Were they there when you woke up?"

"No."

No. They should have been, all of them. The Lady at the very least.

I hesitate. "Were you glad when you woke up?"

"No."

"Why?"

"Because no one else did."

I shift, scoot until ours shoulder touch, my bare arm to his cotton sleeve.

"It was the worst hit on record," he says. "The meteors. The communications tower blew in the first strike. We couldn't get help and flying was dangerous. Not that some didn't try."

He turns our hands until mine is flat under his. Traces my fingertips.

"We were running drills in the city. Guard cadets. Our final infiltration training, that's why we were there. Our instructor, Tevon, handpicked six of us from the academy. It was supposed to be a quick, three-week session. Our parents didn't know."

That's why they weren't there when he woke up.

"We volunteered in fire and rescue. Second strike wiped out half the city. In the third, Tevon had his medichip removed and plugged into me." He laughs, a brittle near-sob. "Rumor was Tevon was a high-level Officiate before taking on our class. Didn't believe it until his chip didn't scan. The medic shredded his shoulder digging it out. But I was the Lord's son, top priority, and required a 'fighting chance.'"

Medichips are supposed to heal anything, up to and including death.

That's what Wren always said.

His hand falls away. "Our service tower was hit two days later. No one else made it out."

I snatch it back, hold it tight to my chest, and try to

channel every warm thing into his open palm.

"But that's enough," I say. His whole arm tenses, starts to pull, but I hold fast. "Maybe you're all that's left, but that's more than enough and if anyone says different, they're wrong."

The mattress shifts, and waxy fingers float along my cheek. "You're crying."

"You know that, right? You *know*?"

The sheets tug and his forehead presses against my temple, but he doesn't answer.

THE BED SHIFTS, THE PILLOW MOVES, AND ITS HEART-
beat disappears. I reach out into warm sheets with no one
in them, which is wrong somehow, but my eyes don't want
to open. A noise, a rustle, a sliding something.

"Eagle?"

His hand is on my ankle. The fingers wrap all the way
around. "Go back to sleep."

"Are we getting up?"

"Just checking something."

"Help?"

The mattress dips and he's closer, leaning in. "What?"

"Need help?"

Nothing. Then, "I've got it."

"Okay."

His fingers trail down my arm and disappear.

I curl into the place where he was.

EIGHT YELLOW CANISTERS HUDDLE NEAR THE scratched hull of Eagle's wing. Their red tops lipstick bright above white scan labels. Eagle crouches on his heels before them, elbows on knees, one thumb tapping his chin.

Eight, not six, and Eagle is decidedly dusty.

"*Why?*" I ask, and he almost falls over. "You went by yourself? There are ghosts down there! You carried two canisters *and* the penlight? I would have—"

"The canisters aren't full," he says. "None of them. Scanned the rest this morning. We don't need to bring the others up."

No, that's not right. Casser wouldn't touch them. They were for Wren.

Wren who was safe in Decontamination, on the moon.

I fight to get the words out. "How short are we?"

"Depends on what fuel we can siphon. Are the base flightwings still here?" He pushes off the ground and stands impossibly straight. Very much the Lord's son.

He's thought about this.

Which means he knows the answer.

"How *short*?"

At his sides, his fingers curl then stretch. "One and a half."

We used half a tank getting here.

"One tank? All those canisters only made one tank?"

He nods.

Which means we just replaced the fuel we burned getting here.

Nothing. This was all for nothing.

"Are there still wings on base?" Eagle asks again.

"They won't help."

"But are they here?"

"Maybe?" I sift through my numb head, held tight between my palms. "Wren's digislate would have a list, it's in her office. Used to be."

"So we go to her office." He strides to the docking bay's entrance.

Everyone will know we're gone by now. They'll come looking. Maybe Dad will stop us at the border if we try to leave.

"Asa?" He waits at the entrance.

"There's nothing left," I say, more to myself than him.

Except he hears.

"You don't know that."

But I do.

EMPTY EYE SOCKETS FIND OUR PENLIGHT IN THE stale dark. Bones in uniforms and street clothes, amid busted courier carts and digislates. Stale, damp, and rancid underneath. Office doors face each other across the chaos, some with personalities intact. Old Mr. Frensis's magnetic welcome sign, Ellena's painted bell-flowers, Pally's hanging fairy with the winged ears.

I speed past, don't look, don't stop.

If I stop, I'll scream.

Wren's door is third from the end, still locked and intact, its access panel blank. Only supplies warranted minisolar circuits, not offices. Eagle pulls out a power pack from his pocket, then a multitool knife. I hold the penlight while he pries off the panel's dusty cover, sorts through wires, and plugs one into the pack. The access screen flickers orange to green, and then reboots.

I scan my palm and key in the override. A low rusty rumble and the door slides slowly open.

Wren's desk faces the door, in perfect alignment with the two silver tube chairs. Datacrecord shelves line the walls, leaving no room for pictures or windows, the brown carpet musty but not decayed.

Almost like nothing happened.

I jerk out of the doorway and heave up my lungs.

"Asa—?"

"Her desk. It's in her desk."

Eagle nods and slips past me through the door. I squeeze my eyes against the hidden bone faces with once happy smiles—all of whom knew me by name.

Carpet-smothered steps. "Okay," Eagle says.

"You found the slate?"

"Yes." He touches my shoulder. "Are you—?"

"I'm coming back." I turn, but the penlight's pointed down and he's just an outline. "Someday I will come back and sing all the House songs and remember because even if they think they're forgotten they're not."

Eagle's hand slips into mine. "I know."

THE TREES ARE DEAD. BLACK SNAKES STANDING SEN-tinel over gape-toothed tower entrances and hollow windows. They used to be brown. Soldiers and biotechnicians would chat below them while the breeze fluttered their silver leaves. I remember.

The trees don't.

Wren's slate has a map, so Eagle doesn't need help finding the base's flightwing hangar. He walks ahead, pace never slowing. Not for the weathered wreck of the research tower or the melted supply warehouse.

Not for the connecting alley between.

Shadows seep from its narrow walls. Hook long fingers under my ribs and *pull*.

I can hear the screams. The echoes, the shouted orders. Everyone wanting something different, Wren's scream loudest of all. *Asa! Get back inside.*

But inside I'd dangled from a fourth-story walkway, while Casser fought through fire and panic to get me down.

Wren grabbed my hand and ran full tilt toward the supply warehouse I'd just gotten free of. I dug in my heels, but she was so *strong*. Strong and deaf through the smoke and blasts, and no matter how much I yelled she didn't hear me.

Or else she wouldn't turn.

She outpaced smoke, skidding us into the warehouse alley, uniform insignia flashing as she spun round.

I cannot deal with you right now, you hear me? I can't. Get back in the damn warehouse and stay until I—

The whole sky whistled.

Wren slammed me to the ground. Broken glass and grated pavement. Curled over me, arms pressing my head into the dirt as the world sparked white.

EAGLE'S SILHOUETTE BLOCKS OUT THE SUN. HE crouches and leans forward enough that I can't see the sky. Dry face, dry fingers. No drips. I reach up, pat his temple and hair. My fingers don't come away red.

"Asa?"

"She knew she wasn't chipped. She was the one who took it out. Maybe she forgot."

Fabric rustles the pavement, and the air shifts to accommodate it. Eagle lies beside me in the dirt. Watches the clouds drift. "Three will get us to Sonnac. We only need a tank and a half."

"Wren chipped the flightwings," I say.

A confused, "What?"

"We didn't have any fuel." I shake my head. That's not right. "I mean, we had a ton of ecoflux from before the factories shut down, just sitting in tanks because all our wings were uleum. Everything was uleum. We hadn't gotten far enough to make new grids yet, which would take old power to build and we didn't have any. Not after quarantine. And we were running out of food, which no one believed because it was Urnath."

He shifts, looks over I think—movement and presence.

"Urnath could grow anything, any season. Nobody went hungry. Not that everyone was safe or healthy or happy, it was just—you could walk out the door and find something to eat. Dad has community farms and orchards on all our planets, but especially here because it was so easy. And if that was too far away, and you took something closer, nobody cared. It'd just grow back in a week or two. And the people who did care, nobody liked them much. It wasn't even theft because there weren't even laws, not for that, not until the Blight. Then everything was poisoned, and we had to fly farther and farther afield to find eatable food. It didn't take long for our uleum to run out. So Wren chipped the wings."

The alley boxes the sky between rooftops. Crisp, stark. I can taste the emptiness.

Eagle half says something, changes his mind, and changes his mind again. "She made them self-healing?" he asks at last, piecing the words together. He's close, almost as close as last night. His face is too much to see all at once.

I rise on my elbows. "No, she made them masking. Medichips work by convincing your body the biotech cells are real, right? That you're running only on your own blood, when you're really not. At least, not wholly."

"Okay?" Slow. He sits up even slower.

"And bodies are a hundred times more complicated then flightwings, right? She just had to make the wings *think* eco-flux was uleum so they would take off."

Eagle shakes his head. "But it's a completely different tech."

"No, it's a *story*. Wren could do anything. You should see the models she built for her tech classes."

"But the fuels aren't compatible. Even if the wings booted, they wouldn't fly."

"Yes, they would. They *did*." I sit, too.

He waits, waits, and watches, hand splayed on the ground near my thigh.

I rub my neck. "Okay, so they only lasted a few flights, four tops, but that was four shipments more than we had."

"Then what?"

"The engines blew."

"So you had no wings."

"We had nothing!" I push onto my feet, away from the grit and rugged ache. "Don't you see? It'd been months and there was nothing left. Maybe we lost the wings and maybe half the shipments were Blighted by that point, but at least it was *something*."

Look. Wren held out the bloodied medichip she'd had the lieutenant so carefully remove. *This is our truth and we're going to make it stick.*

And she did. *We* did. Casser never caught on, or the flight crews. Wren rewrote schematics and hacked together duplicate chips to wire into the engines. I broke all the measurement gauges on the uleum tanks so no one could see how little we had. We told them all we had enough for the next flight, and then we made it true.

My breath dissipates. Balances.

I am a Daughter of Fane. My truth and my story.

Wren's medichip would make it stick.

She wired it into her wing, but I could get it out.

"You have Wren's digislate?" I ask.

He stands and pulls the slate from his pocket. Holds it out. I tap through the menus and access Wren's research files and diagrams. Everything labeled with full sidebars of notes.

"She could remap me," I whisper. My whole body's a whisper.

"What?"

The medichip file unpacks layer after layer of biocell programs, schematics, and tests—the final perfect combination that made ecoflux look like uleum.

That could make me look like I'm Dad's.

"Wren can mask me!" I hand the slate to Eagle, bounce onto my toes. "We'd need a control point to copy, so we'd have to visit Wren, and of course, we'd need the medichip from her wing."

He scrolls through, tapping notes and scanning lines. "Asa—"

"You're not seeing it." I point at the screen. "If we get the chip, we just have to hook it up to the slate. The schematic will do everything else. It was easy, I watched Wren. We just need to copy her blood signature and—"

"No." Eagle switches the slate off, as if that's the end of it.

Which it absolutely is not.

"But she could prove *me*," I say.

"No." The slate disappears into his pocket. "The engines blew. You said."

"So will everything! All of Fane's planets are uleum-rich. We have enough to last Galton decades, and Mom knows it. We'll be leveled like the independents, and everywhere will turn into *this*." I fling out my arms. "*This* is what a dead planet looks like. And even if they don't invade, if you're blood bonded to Galton, do you think they'll let your dad ever send the food?"

"No."

"And it's my fault! I did this, Eagle. *Me*. I drugged Emmie. I tied you and your House to somebody who isn't even *real*. I could have found another way to save Wren, snuck her out of the medicenter or *something*. But no, I went and married us in an impossible bond and I'd give anything to take it back."

The words echo. Split like shrapnel and scatter.

"Well," says Eagle, one harsh line from head to foot. "You can't."

"I know." Blood bright and lost between tears I can't stop. "I'm sorry."

Eagle doesn't move.

I press my fisted hands to my forehead, and *order* my eyes clear. When I finally look up, Eagle is still there.

He holds out his hand.

And I take it.

EAGLE WON'T LISTEN. WE COMB THE BASE FOR FUEL-filled, nonchipped wings that don't exist, and he still won't listen. He keeps pointing out how the flightwings blew up.

Like he gets to decide.

He sprawls across the bed, hasn't moved his head since it hit the pillow. Bare feet dangling, arm brushing the dipped sheets where I was when he laid down.

Where I won't be when he wakes up.

I lean over the mattress on tiptoe, lay his digislate near his head. A note will pop up as soon as he turns it on, saying that I'm with Wren and he should go home.

Wren's wing should still fly. It's not big enough to haul supplies, and she only took it out twice, postchipping. It'll get me to Malsa. It's not far, only a couple planets over.

I slip his jacket off the hook and slide it over my shoulders. With the hood up, no one will know me.

With the hood up, I can close my eyes and breathe him in.

BLOOD

'M A GHOST. I FLOAT UNCHALLENGED PAST THE HAR-ried flight coordinator who isn't Casser and doesn't know my voice. Coast into the medicenter's docking bay, despite the myriad flashing gauges. Don't crash. Drift into the stormy gray of the coma ward. Nara rushes by checking her digislate, Gregor pushes his cart between rooms, and Kelie argues into central reception's deskcom.

I approach Wren's door by stages, wait for an unwatched moment, then scan my hand and slip inside. Gently close it behind me. Lean my forehead against the door.

Eagle's probably up by now. Reading the note. Flying home.

I exhale everything in me. "Hey, Wren."

"Asa."

My heart hits the ceiling as my feet leave the floor.

Dad. Messy, actually messy with bunched sleeves and dark circles under his eyes, like the universe disappeared and left him behind.

And took Wren with it.

"No!" I run to the bed, hood falling back as I grab her

slack fingers with one hand and press the other to her heart. "No, please, no. Dad? Is she?"

But her chest rises. The monitor beeps. Her limp fingers aren't frozen or soulless, just chilled from being too long above the blankets.

My head drops as my arms stretch, locked over her hand and heart.

"Okay. It's okay. You have to stick with me," I say for her or Dad or both. "I've been looking up specialists in Westlet, and you have to stick with me until I can figure it out."

Dad fixates on my blonde head, but says only, "Give me your hand."

I reach out automatically. He turns it palm up and pushes up my sleeve. Places a flat black circle on my wrist. It feels like metal. And writhes. I jerk, but Dad holds fast as the disc morphs into two expanding bands that snap around my wrist.

I've never seen a retrieval wristlet up close, though the Enforcers on base always carried them. A tracker for those awaiting judgment, it incapacitates if tampered with or if the timer runs out before removal.

The embedded digiscreen flashes once, twice, then projects a small holorecord onto my palm.

The countdown.

The numbers fuzz at the edges. "A retrieval wristlet?"

I ask.

"I've guaranteed your appearance. The wristlet shows when and where. I'll send a transport. Until then, you can stay here."

It takes forever to lift my head. To meet Dad's eyes.

He knew I'd come. That's why he's here.

"You said I couldn't be tested."

"I said I would handle it, and now I have no options." He cuts himself off, then adds a careful, "Apparently, your mother fears for your life. Due to your disappearance, it is only natural that I intend to slit your throat and incinerate your body so the treaty can never be disproved."

"That's—nobody would believe that!"

"It's your mother." He moves around the bed, toward the door. "Where do you think you get your 'stories' from?"

Not harsh or grated or even disappointed. Only fact.

I wind my fingers through Wren's. She doesn't grip back. Behind me, the door opens.

"I wouldn't worry over much, Dad," I say, just loud enough to hear. "You never believe mine."

Only the monitor answers. Four beeps, five.

And the door clicks shut behind him.

"HOW COULD YOU BE SO STUPID?" EMMIE'S BOOTED heels pound out periods beyond Wren's bed. Dad must have told her I was here because she came soon after he left. "And what is up with your hair?"

I lean against the bed rails, which are cool and level and don't rise to the bait. "I dyed it."

"I can see that." Emmie is red lipstick and poise, backed by white walls that seem to shy away from her. "Did you even consider the rest of us? What would happen if you disappeared?"

"Did I think Genevieve would say Dad murdered me? No! I didn't!"

"Then you should have."

I push off hard enough that the bed scrapes. I rush to check Wren's monitor and pulse. "Sorry, I'm sorry."

"You should be," says Emmie.

"That wasn't for you."

"No, of course not." Emmie kicks at the wall, cheeks bright, and I can't tell if it's her or her makeup. "It never is."

"You stole the schematics!"

"And you stole the *alliance*."

Outside, the birds scatter and I want to fly off with them.

"I'm sorry." I straighten the bed, smooth the covers, and add, "Emmie," in case she doesn't know.

She stares out the window. "You know Wren won't wake up."

"Don't say that." I lean close to Wren. "Don't listen, she doesn't mean it."

"I've had them run all the tests. Again."

"That was you?" I move around the bed to the window, where the sky bleeds orange. "What did they say?"

"What they always say—that she's not waking up." Emmie jams her hair behind her ear. "You're going to have to face it sooner or later, preferably not at the expense of our House."

"But those are our scans."

She droops forward, bumps her head against the glass.

I scoot closer. "No, listen. Westlet has this advanced treatment that I really think—"

"Of course, you do." She takes my shoulders. "Asa, you really, really have to get it together. I know you miss her, but this?" Her head jerks at the bed. "This is no life. It's not fair, but nothing is."

"I know."

Every raw thing inside me knows, and saps my strength away.

But it can't. I have to fix the treaty and get Wren to Westlet and—

And.

Emmie pulls me into a hug. Wraps me in gingernut and confidence until my eyes ache. "Don't get soggy on me. I'm going to handle everything."

"You can't. It's not your fault." I bury my face in her hair.

She rubs my back. "I've already shown Dad the tests, and I'm thinking we can pull her next week. You don't even have to be here—"

"What?" I yank away, step back and back again. "What?"

"You knew this was coming! I wanted to have it done and over before you came back so you wouldn't have to deal with it."

And I would have lost my chance to say goodbye.

"Out." I point at the door, arm thrumming. "Out."

"Seriously? Come on—"

"No." I march close and push her across the room, her boots slide-clacking with her protests. I open the door and slam it locked behind her.

"Asa!" Muffled with her pounding fist. "Asa, what are you doing?"

I slide to the floor, wrap my arms around my legs and bawl.

THE MEDICHIP DANGLES WIRES AND DUST. A FLAT rectangle as long as my smallest nail, but not so wide. Fragile and almost impossible to find, even with Wren's notes. After cleaning myself up, I spliced it out of the console. Her flightwing is officially dead now.

Not that it wasn't anyway.

The medichip shouldn't dangle anything. It didn't when Wren took it out, and doesn't in the initial diagrams on her slate. She built schematics based in biotech first, detailing the masking in the original environment. Then once it worked in program, she translated it into fuel and engines.

I sit cross-legged on the bed and tie Wren's blood signature into the final bio-based schematic. When I asked Aston for another signature, he retrieved it with no more than a, *yes, m'lady.*

All the medics get like that after Dad visits.

I hold the slate up for Wren to see. Wren, who could have been dead right now.

No, stop. Medichip first.

"What do you think?"

Nothing, not even mountains.

"That's not helpful," I say.

Which isn't fair. Dad revoked my End-Level network access, but not Wren's. Or at least, not her all-levels-cleared digislate with palm print access. All I had to do to find the stabilized ecoflux schematic was place her hand on the screen.

Maybe she figures that's help enough.

The embedded wall-com near her monitor flashes blue. I tap the screen. "Yeah?"

"A visitor, m'lady," says Nara through the speaker. "One of our Lady's soldiers, I think."

From Urnath. They still visit sometimes, mostly if they're being transferred or moving away. When they don't plan on coming back.

I trace my palm's tiny, marching numbers.

"Should I send him on his way, m'lady?" Nara asks.

Yes.

Except he's probably flying out tonight.

"No. She'll see him." I stow Wren's chip and slate in the small stand by the bed. Cross the room and open the door.

Eagle.

Hoodless in a smudged gray shirt and glaring fire.

"You're here!" I spring forward, throw my arms around his neck. "Why are you here? You're supposed to be home."

He glances down the hall, slips inside and kicks the door closed. Then he takes my shoulders, more vibration than shake. "You can't do that, Asa. You can't."

Oh. Right.

I step back, hug his jacket instead of him.

Except it just pushes the splinters deeper.

"Yeah. I know. I didn't mean—" But I did. It takes everything I have not to reach out again. I hold up my wrist instead. "Dad put a tracker on me. There's no running now. Go home."

He snatches my hand and examines it between both of his. Tests the wristlet and rubs the countdown with his thumb, holo sliding over his skin as he fingerprints my being. "You're his *daughter*."

"You need to go home. Please."

His hold tightens. "You weren't there. I woke up and you weren't there."

"I have to fix it."

"Without me?"

"Not if you'd *listen*." I mean to let go, but my stupid fingers squeeze instead. "You don't know Wren, but I *do*. Even her worst prototypes since we were little—all of them worked even when they broke. Dad couldn't get ecoflux off the ground until Wren started messing with it. This will work, too."

"It will kill you."

"It won't."

"If. It. Does?"

"Then that's *my* chance and *my* choice." I tug my hand free. "You don't get to say."

He fills the gap. "We're blood bonded. I get a say."

"You don't even want me to hug you!" The words fill almost as much space as he does. There's no way to take them back. To erase the surprised shift of his expression, the shock I can almost taste.

"Never mind. Forget it. Go home." I step back.

He steps with me. Hands catching my cheeks, closing in until the room disappears and I taste *him*. Wide lips and lost places. Tangled forests of pine nuts and rivers and the way the air sings before the sun rises. His fingers chase dawn into my hair. I rise up on my toes, and my heart speeds so fast through the branches I'd swear I'm lost, except I feel it. Every beat. Against his chest.

"I'm not leaving," he whispers.

I burrow into him and bury my face in his shirt. "Then trust me."

His arms wrap tight but he doesn't say anything, not even *no*.

I look up, but he stares across the room. At Wren.

"We'll need a chip implanter," he says.

EAGLE LOCKS ALL HIS WING'S DOORS, SEALS OFF THE
cockpit, then blazes the lights. The docking bay is tied to
the medicenter, which is where the wristlet will say I am.

I scroll through the menu screen of the medi-
implanter—not chip specific, but workable. It worked for
Wren. Blue and red with a slotted mouth on one end and a
handle on the other, a full color digiscreen between. It also
works as a scanner, so I can program depth and location.
The implanter will beep until it's in the right spot.

I borrowed it from the tech lab. Hopefully Nara won't
need it tonight.

Wren's slate glows numbers and I plug them all in.
Double-check everything. "Okay," I say, looking up. "I just
need the chip and—"

He's half-naked. Face and arms lost in the shirt he is
pulling over his head. White and yellow light battle warm
undertones over his deep brown skin—rivulets and oceans
drifting down his chest. Then his shirt hits the floor and he's
staring back.

"What are you doing?" I ask. Don't squeak. Mostly.

He swipes Wren's chip from the table and stuffs it in the
wall garbage chute.

"No!" I shoot forward, but he slams the *empty* button. The chute shudders, wheezes. Shredding our Houses,
the treaty.

Me.

And Eagle reaches for his jacket like it's of no consequence at all.

I grab Wren's slate and head to the door.

"Asa."

"You said you trusted me." I jab at the door's security panel. "You *said*."

Except he hadn't. Not specifically. I'd just assumed, because—

Because.

I unlock the door, and then Eagle's hand is there, holding it shut.

"We use mine," he says.

"You have a medichip lying around and didn't tell me?"

Eagle hefts his jacket and empties its pockets on the table. Gauze, disinfectant packets, tweezers.

Surgical knives. Two. Shiny, sterile, and clattering. In my ears, under my skin.

My hand slips from the panel. "No."

"Chips have to acclimate," he says. "Mine can handle a transfer and wasn't wired for an engine."

"No."

"It's safe. Safer."

I carefully lay Wren's digislate on the table, as far from the knives as possible. "Shredded. You said his shoulder was shredded."

"Mine won't be," Eagle says like there's no question.

"Yes. It will."

He steps close, too bare and too stark. "It won't."

"Eagle, *no*."

He skims rough palms over my shoulders, like *I'm* the one about to be hacked to pieces. "Trust me."

"I'll hit something vital."

"In my shoulder?"

"It'll scar."

"Not an issue."

"Eagle—"

His breath warms my nose and lips. "Asa."

And everything there is to say, he says with my name.

We're the treaty. Us. Just us. Our responsibility. *My* responsibility.

We've started, now we stick.

Eagle moves a chair around the table and sits with his back to me. Rubs his left shoulder. "This one."

On this side, the skin's smooth, seamless, nothing to say where the chip is or isn't. But it shouldn't be deep. Wren's wasn't. It'll be small, tiny, like a splinter. I used to dig out splinters for the soldiers on base with a stitching needle. It wasn't so bad. They didn't flinch.

Much.

I grab the implanter, find the SCAN option and move it back and forth above his shoulder. It doesn't blink green or beep. It doesn't register anything.

Of course not. He said it didn't scan. And this implanter probably wouldn't recognize chips anyway.

Eagle half turns toward me.

"Do you remember?" I ask. "Where they chipped you?"

His right hand drifts over his shoulder until his finger-tips slide past his armpit to the section between his side and spine. "In here. I think."

Pure, unbroken skin.

I search the area, pressing hard and circling out. He's warm, almost hot.

"You won't feel it." His voice lacks the tension I can feel in his skin. "The medics didn't."

"Right." I grab a swab packet from the table and disin-fect his skin. "You didn't grab pain pills or anything? Like a numbing agent?"

He shakes his head.

I'm going to be sick.

Fane doesn't get sick.

I return the packet, take the smallest knife—razor-edged with a plain white handle. "Ready?"

"Shoot." Fraying. A little, enough.

I'm taking too long, and making it worse.

My hands shake, but there isn't time for that or anything else. I push everything out of my head. Keep the knife steady.

Focus.

The blade bites.

He tenses, blood wells, hurricanes scream in my ears but not my hands because I need to be steady and smooth. One slice down, another across. His skin gives like putty, dripping red lines down his back.

Eagle doesn't make a sound.

I'm not sick, can't be, *won't*.

I carefully lay the knife on the table—or mean to, but I let go too quickly and it clatters down, scattering blood. Eagle jumps. I grab the tweezers.

This needs to be over. Now, fast, yesterday.

I HAVE TO DIG.

The first cuts are not deep enough and in the wrong spots and blood fills the widening gaps and muddles everything and his knuckles glow on the chair and my cheeks are as soaked as my red, red fingers and his breath's heavy and mine hiccups and beyond that neither of us makes a sound.

THE CHIP PINGS AGAINST THE TABLETOP, BLEEDS RED glue. I grab all the gauze I can find, and press it tightly to his shoulder. Blood seeps and drains and it doesn't help that my shaky hands are as sticky as the wound.

"Eagle?" High, off-balance.

A thick, hoarse, "Yeah?"

"I need you to hold this. I—I've got to get the kit."

Slowly he reaches across and over his shoulder, finds the gauze.

I let go and bolt the two steps to the cabinet near the cockpit, yank it open, and grab his wing's emergency kit from the top shelf. Haul it back to the table and dig. My fingers print everything red but it doesn't matter and I don't care because here's more gauze and sealant and stronger, thicker bandages.

I clean his blood away, press the seams together before too much more ebbs out, squeeze sealant along the lines. Cover everything with gauze and tape until his shoulder is a padded mountain. His breath evens out, almost steadies.

I should ask how he feels. Move around and check his face to see the damage I've done, but the answer is crusted on my fingertips. The room spins, overbright, my head is a disconnected bubble. I reach soft, softly for the shoulder I haven't mauled. Rest my forehead against his hair without pressing too close. He smells like exhaustion and woods and firelight and it's so impossibly hard to move.

But I have to. He needs meds. And better bandages. And fresh gauze and sealant and disinfectant and none of those things will magically appear.

"Can you stand?" I ask. "I'll get the bed down."

His hand finds mine. Clasps my wrist and tugs until I move around the chair, his eyes hollow etches of hurt.

"I'm sorry," I say, as if that makes up for anything. "It'll only take a second, I'll move the chair back and you can sit while I—"

He pulls and keeps pulling until I sink into his lap.

"Eagle." I try to rise without shifting or hurting him but his arm's an anchor, holding me close. As if my strength will feed his. Except I haven't any.

If I did, I wouldn't bury my face in the warm safety of his neck and press my hand to his heart to make sure it's still beating.

We sit a long, long time.

THE IMPLANTER GLOWS BLUE IN EAGLE'S HAND. WE sit side by side on the bed. Remapping was easy. Put the chip in the implanter, connect the implanter to Wren's digislate. Load the updated schematic tied to her blood. Reboot the chip. Take it out then put it back in to make sure the schematic stuck. Apparently, I'll need time to acclimate.

Eagle needs time to acclimate. I'm not sure how he's sitting up.

"Ready?" he asks.

I climb onto the bed and sit facing the wall. Pull off my shirt and fold it in my lap. My back feels as raw as my scrubbed hands.

As long as it's going into me, not him, it's okay.

The stuffy air stretches across my skin, promising bites that don't come.

I half turn. "Eagle?"

His gaze jumps from my back to me then away. Two blinks, less than a second.

I face forward, hands overhot and clutching my shirt.

The mattress slopes as Eagle balances on his knees behind me. He slips my bra strap over my shoulder, smooths the area where the chip will go. "It's quick. There's a numbing agent."

The implanter eats the warmth away. The drifting metal

mouth *beep beep beeps* over my skin, until it finds the place it wants. The beeps morph into one solid tone.

"Okay?" he asks.

I nod.

Cold barrels through my skin and explodes fire. A scream rips from nowhere, jerked short by my constricted throat, which won't open. I curl forward, bend double.

The chip crawls. A beetle. A living, multilegged beetle burrowing deep bloody dens.

"Asa?"

My forehead's on the mattress.

"Asa, what's wrong?"

The chip twists and writhes and I won't scream anymore I won't *I won't.*

Except fire spreads. I jerk but the beetle panics in all the wrong directions and *digs.*

I'm screaming or someone's screaming and there's blood on my tongue and under my skin and between the beetle's teeth and—

"Asa!"

Nothing. There's nothing.

I can't feel anything.

Eagle's saying something, a lot of somethings. He's close, head and chest curled over me. Maybe arms and hands. I can't feel him.

"Your shoulder," I say against the muffling sheets. "Let me go. You'll mess it up."

"Asa?"

"I used up all the gauze. You'll bleed through." I push myself away, up the bed. At least, I think I'm moving.

"It shouldn't have done that." Eagle sinks beside me instead of staying still like he should. The bandages will break and I can't feel my fingers to fix them. "The numbing should be instant. I remember. Something's wrong. Something's really wrong. We have to get it out."

"No." I reach up, grab his wrist with all my strength. Except I miss, and my fingers won't close.

He keeps moving. "Stay still, I'll—"

"*No*," I yell, try to, wavering desperation. It takes the last of my air. "Please. I didn't cut you open for nothing. Don't make that for nothing."

He freezes, maybe, I think, and leans close. But it's too dark to see, and I can't hear anymore.

THE WRISTLET BUZZES UP MY ARM AND DOWN THE sheets. The ceiling blazes, every light on and blinding. Eagle's close, on his stomach, arm across my waist. I check his shoulder. The bandage is messy and somewhat twisted but not red. The sealant worked. I sink back, lifting my wrist. Read the floating text on my palm.

TRANSPORT IN TWO HOURS. PLEASE PREPARE.

My arm drops to the bed.

"How long?" Eagle's eyes are open, more awake than his words.

"Two hours. Dad's sending a transport."

He nods.

"Will the chip acclimate by then?"

Eagle rises enough to check the digiclock above the cockpit door, then pulls me a little closer. "I don't know. Mine didn't hurt."

"Neither does mine." Now. I can't feel it.

Actually, I can't feel much on that side.

"Shoulder?" he asks.

I reach for his bandage, trace the edge. "I don't think it bled through, is the pain bad?"

He scrunches his nose into the sheets. "*Yours*, not mine."

"Mine wasn't shredded."

"I'm fine," he says.

The wristlet buzzes. I shake my arm and check the

band. "You told me that already."

Eagle raises his arm then taps the band until the text changes in acknowledgment. He tugs at its smooth edge, as if there's room for his fingers to slide under. "This is coming off."

"Don't mess with it, the drug will activate." I place his arm back where it was. It is rippled and warm and very, very still.

"What drug?" he asks.

"To knock me out if I don't show. It's a retrieval wristlet."

"You said it was a tracker."

"It is."

"With a drugging agent."

"It's fine."

"No, it's not," he says into my neck. Then his lips stay, just stay, not quite touching.

"Eagle?"

"Hmm?"

"Are you okay? Really?"

His arm tightens. "Yeah. You?"

I nod. We're lying, but if we both know maybe it doesn't count.

"Eagle?"

"Yeah?"

"I want to bring Wren home."

"What?" He raises his head.

"I don't know which medicenter," I say. "I haven't researched enough. But there are more treatments in Westlet and new things we haven't tried and she's so far away now."

His expression is a spun balance of this or that and too much of both.

"Home," he repeats.

"I know there's not a lot of hope, but there's some. Enough not to give up yet." The tears press and expand and I let them fall. "And if, *if* it turns out there isn't any, then maybe she could come to the main complex? For a week or two? So she isn't alone?"

"I'll tell Father."

"And you're really okay? You'd tell me?"

He eases back down and kisses my jaw.

"That better mean yes."

"Yes," he says.

GAMES

THE WESTLET CAPITAL IS A FOREST WITH SKY-towers folded in. Trees own the city—some impossibly tall—leaves green between sun-kissed buildings that curve like branches from a spiral. There's no high-level wing traffic, no winking ad-screens. No hint the buildings breathe.

Even SolTech tower, the official headquarters of Mekenna Solis's biotechnology, seemed abandoned from the air. Inside, people bustle in lab coats past blue wall-screens with office itineraries.

The windows encompass the hall from the docking bay and I wish Eagle would come back. He asked me to wait, but somebody passed by a second ago and now people peer around corners. No one's supposed to know why I'm here, but they all know who I am.

The medichip hasn't scratched more holes under my skin, so I must be acclimating. Even if my bones feel strung with string.

I smooth my cuff over the wristlet. Dad sent clothes with the transport. Functional more than frilly, but definitely

House. White slacks and shirt, with a thin brown band high on each sleeve. There were even a few suits for Eagle in different sizes, tagged with, *In case the boy is with you.* Not proper Westlet colors with embroidered cuffs—Dad wouldn't have access to those—but formal dark neutrals that promise power without spelling it out. I helped Eagle into the one shirt that fit.

Eagle had to sit down. I thought he was going to pass out. Maybe he has. I rebandaged his shoulder, but maybe it bled through. Maybe—

Brisk echoes and there he is, rounding the corner down the hall. Very much the soldier in deep gray, boots gleaming with the floor.

Dad is with him. Compact edges and heavy tread, messiness gone.

Eagle sweeps the corridor until the peering faces disappear, then says, "Take it off."

I lift my wrist and Dad presses his thumb to the band. The gelled metal morphs back into a solid disc, and he palms it into a pocket. Eagle weaves his fingers through mine, his eyes on Dad.

Neither say a word.

I squeeze Eagle's hand. "After."

They can not-yell at each other after.

He squeezes back, but tells Dad, "This doesn't happen again."

"She is my daughter." A statement, not a paternity claim. I rub my chest against the burn, but it doesn't matter. I'll make it true anyway.

"*Asa*," Eagle says, "is the Lady of this House."

Not *future*, just Lady, as if the office is already mine. Because it is. Will be.

The hall shifts and I brace against the full weight of what that *means*. What Wren woke up every day knowing. What Eagle must have as well. That one day, every House responsibility will come down to them, whether they are ready or not.

Now it's down to me. Us. Here.

I rise up on tiptoe and kiss Eagle's jaw.

"Baby!" calls a bright someone and I jump out of my skin.

Lady Galton dances forward, sunny hair wafting over purple silk. Her nails are indigo, her scent lilac—her graceful arms flying around my neck. "My beautiful, beautiful daughter. I was so worried! Are you well? Let me look at you."

She's everywhere, hand slipping between mine and Eagle's, tugging me down the hall. Fingers fluttering over my cheeks like maybe I'm not real. "I was so worried. You have no idea."

"You had no reason." I pull away and Dad's hand appears in my peripheral, on my shoulder, before she can reclaim me. I can't feel it.

His pale knuckles say that's a good thing.

"Lady Galton."

I was wrong. Dad never once swore with my name. Not like that.

Her smile turns phosphorescent. "I'd like a moment with my daughter."

"That would be a first."

"And you would know that, how?" A more-ness slips into her voice, history and depth, and the air skitters between them. In the same room, almost sharing the same breath, they're the twisted inverse of Wren and Emmie. Everything wrong and right and broken, and I slide away before they break me, too.

"I'm ready," I say. "Let's go."

EAGLE OPENS THE DOOR AND THE ROOM STUTTERS. The Triplicate's here, all of them. Multihued iridescence amid the nondescript couches of a formal discussion room. Lady Westlet in deep orange to the Lord's silver. Genevieve's purple sparkle floating to confer with Lord Galton's waiting blue.

Dad in unbroken brown to my encompassing white. As if we are Lord and Heir, not Lord and youngest. I hadn't noticed, getting dressed.

Everyone notices now.

"Darling." Lady Westlet steps forward in an asymmetrical dress that scorns sparkle, and kisses my cheek. "Welcome to Mekenna's labs. Charming, aren't they? She's promised us a full tour once the matter is sorted."

"My Lady," I say.

She pats my shoulder and moves to kiss Eagle with a razor smile. "My, don't you look well? Though House colors might have been appropriate."

Eagle stares straight ahead.

"It was what he had," I say, instead of, *then you should have brought him some.*

The thought must come through anyway, for the Lady only says, "Ah."

"Speaking of sorted." Genevieve threads an arm around my waist and pulls me toward the man who is absolutely not my dad. "Shall we get that out of the way first?"

"It would be about time." Lord Galton takes my chin between three fingers and tips my head back. His round face matches his round vowels and square, digging fingertips.

Genevieve touches his wrist. "Remember what she is. Punctuality can be taught."

"Yes," he says. "It will."

No, it won't.

I pull back and smack into a wall.

Or rather Eagle, who reaches for my arm and holds tight.

His *shoulder*. I can't make him sit down or check the sealant or yell because everyone's watching.

So I ease away and ask, "Where is the test?"

"Here." The Lady sweeps in and directs me toward the only non-House individual in the room. "Mekenna has everything set up."

Mekenna has replaced her glitter earrings for simple studs that match her noncommittal suit. She nods a formal greeting, then pulls a green disc from her pocket. "The other signatures have already been drawn, m'lady. Yours will conclude the test."

She presses the disc's center. It jumps, glows white, and floats above her palm. Stays airborne as she removes her hand. "Lay your wrist on the hover, please."

I do as told, tugging up my sleeve, arm outstretched. The hover hums, static energy locking my arm in place. Binding my wrist steady even as my body shivers.

Mekenna next takes a shiny black thing from an end table. "This evaluation is for parentage only. Any viral anomalies outside the defined zone will not be shared or recorded. The results will forward automatically to a secure deposit in the greater House network, where they cannot be deleted, overwritten, or tampered with."

"Sweet Mekenna," says Lady Galton. "So efficient."

The shiny thing turns out to be two metal strips, crossed at the center, that curve down into four even legs. Mekenna settles it on the hover so the crosshairs pin my pulse. The legs lock and a mini 3-D holorecord appears, zipping through a stream of text before ending with, *Initiation complete. Activate when ready.*

Mekenna taps the reader and a needle spears. I jerk.

"Easy." She holds my palm flat while metal slits its way down and down, and holo letters spin.

It doesn't hurt, not actual pain. Just presence. A thirsty pull under my skin, in my blood. Like the medichip.

Which has absolutely, positively acclimated.

Compiling . . . flashes the holo text. *Compiling* . . . *Compiling* . . .

Wrinkles skitter across Mekenna's face. She releases my

palm, flips her hand, and taps the crosshairs of the reader with one hard knuckle. The needle burrows until my stomach stings.

Flash flash flash.

"What's taking so long?" Lord Galton asks. "Mine was instantaneous."

"No doubt due to your thick veins," says Lady Westlet.

"The *transmission* is instant, my Lord," Mekenna says, "not necessarily the—"

Parentage compiled, reads the holo. *Subject 3 child of Subject 1. Transmitting results.*

The needle disappears.

Genevieve glows. "That would be Jaered, yes?"

I shake my head. Eagle's blood is on my hands and under my nails and that will *not* be for nothing.

"No," I tell the reader, the floating text, the entire room. "It's Dad."

"If by 'Dad' you mean Lord Fane," says Mekenna, "then yes. He was the first subject."

The world stalls between heartbeats. Suspended as my wrist, my blood, my dizzy head.

Dad's. I'm Dad's.

"What?" barks Lord Galton.

"Oh, what a lot of fuss." Lady Westlet says, tumbled as her smile. "Now, Mekenna, dear, how about that tour you so beautifully promised."

"Of course, my Lady." Mekenna reaches for the reader, but Lord Galton grabs her wrist. "Test again."

I try to pull free of the reader, but the energy field holds me in place.

Mekenna pastes on a smile. "The results are sent, my Lord. They cannot be overwritten."

"And if they've done something to her? Given her one of your famous blood chips? Test again."

She stares pointedly at his locked fingers. "Medichips heal. They do not rewrite DNA."

Lord Galton lets go and taps the reader. The initiation text appears and he pounds the crosshairs with two harsh fingers, sinking the needle so deep into my wrist it almost spears the hover. I scream.

Eagle barrels into Galton and they disappear from view.

Compiling . . . compiling . . .

An end table crashes, followed by a harsh, "You *dare*?"

Flash flash flash.

Severed skin and fire and of course the needle hasn't punctured my wrist, not all the way through, that's stupid, it can't have.

My arm might fall off.

"Stand down," says Lord Westlet from somewhere, chased by the Lady's, "Eagle!" and Dad's, "Enough."

And rising over it all, "Results inconclusive. Please retest."

Genevieve stands at my shoulder, pointing at the holorecord above my screaming wrist. My head swims and the letters fuzz, but they don't rearrange.

Lord Galton's finger points with his wife's in unmitigated triumph. "And what do you say now?"

"No," I say.

It's wrong. It has to be. The chip acclimated. It *worked*.

Except the holo doesn't change and I can't see Eagle.

Mekenna's brow knots as she reaches for my wrist.

"Decontamination," I rush out. "It's because of Decontamination."

"What?" asks Genevieve.

"Asa," Dad warns.

He should know me better.

"Wren blew up her lab once, with us in it," I say, because it's true and as good a place to start as any. "One of her chemical experiments went wrong. The fire wasn't so bad, but the fumes were awful—so slimy you could actually *feel* them—and we got sick. Really sick." I look over my shoulder at Dad. "Remember that summer Wren kept me on Urnath? And she kept dreaming up excuses why we couldn't come home yet? That was why. We had to flush the chemicals out, and Wren didn't want you to know." My wrist hurts and my arm and I refocus on Mekenna. "It worked, we got better, but her eye color changed twice and my toenails fell off and never grew back. Here, you can see." I reach for my shoes, but lightning shoots up my wrist and through my head and my legs buckle.

Genevieve catches me as the room upends. "Get it off, just get it off her."

But Mekenna's already deactivating the reader, retracting the needle. The crosshairs disengage, then the energy field, and my wrist slides off the hover. I clutch it to my chest.

"Genevieve," says Lord Galton.

"You've proven the point," she says. "Oh God, she's bleeding. Here, baby, let me see."

I hug my arm tighter, take a shaky step back. "I'm fine, it's fine."

Lord Galton snakes around Mekenna to grab my arm. "No, you're not done yet."

"You *cannot* be serious." Lord Westlet appears behind Galton a second before Eagle does, blocking his path. The room shrinks, condenses, the world boiling over.

"Baby, your blouse is red, you have to let me see."

"She needs a blood chip scan. Now."

"My Lord, as I said, a medichip can't—"

"*Can't?* You're sure you are fully cognizant of all technological advances in the thirteen years of their lockdown? I want her scanned."

"No." Dad.

"Asa." Eagle.

"*You* do not get a say in this." Galton.

"Sweetie, if you would let me—" Genevieve.

"*Enough*," I yell. Loud. It echoes. I raise my head. "Scan me."

I SIT ON THE BED, MY BACK TO THE OBSERVATION WINdow, but it doesn't matter. I feel them, their eyes. Watching.

The small lab tastes of scrubbed steel and stars. Gray floor washed silver in the overheads. Mekenna stands at the deep counter built into the opposite wall, pulling packets from this drawer, filling a glass from the sink, dropping something into the water.

"Drink this."

Clear bubbles float and pop between things that squiggle.

"It's for the scan," she says.

Which I asked for.

I gulp it down. Mildew slimes down my throat and I cough. Mekenna sweeps the glass away, then takes my wrist without preamble and cleans the blood. Swift, efficient strokes that burn. I grab the bed's edge with my free hand and don't pass out.

Barely.

"That was interesting." She rips open a packet, removes a transparent sealant square and smooths it over my wrist. "I would have said impossible."

"What is?"

"An inconclusive signature from someone who *isn't* newly chipped."

Breathe, just breathe.

"It happens to me all the time," I say. "At home."

"Again, interesting." Mekenna cleans up the packet and dabbing cloth, rinses out the glass. Then she returns and jabs an injector pen into my wrist.

I yelp.

"For pain." She steadies my hand with careful fingers that don't match her eyes. "So what exactly were you contaminated with?"

"I don't know? Wren called it the Bug."

Which is sort of true. That's what Wren first called the Blight, before it destroyed the farms.

I sway, but there's nothing to keep me steady and upright—except Mekenna.

"And you lost your toenails," she states, as if she's pegged the lie I can't talk my way out of.

I kick off a shoe, reach down to slip off my sock. Stubby toes with bare gaps. At least they don't have those weird green threads anymore.

Mekenna's mouth curves on an *oh*, but all she says is, "Lie down, please."

I do, scooting back on the slick metal surface. There's no mattress, but the chip hasn't acclimated enough for my back to feel things yet.

Just as long as it doesn't matter for the scan.

The ceiling tiles are locked white squares.

More opening drawers, metal clattering.

"This is a live scan. All information will be streamed to the holo in the observation window."

Mekenna lines a series of discs along the counter and activates them one by one. They spring into the air. Skitter to float above my head in a long glowing line. Then they lock together and beam white. Scan me up and down in a regulated march. Two passes, five.

Then the beam cuts out and the discs cluster. Mekenna pulls them from the air.

Shouts rise beyond the observation window, indistinguishable through the pane.

Don't react. Whatever she says, don't be surprised and don't react.

"It seems you're not chipped." Mekenna opens a drawer and tosses in the discs.

I loosen, almost float. "I told you."

"Of course, any biotechnician worth her salt intent on building untraceable medichips would program them to *be* untraceable—even by her own scanners." Mekenna reaches across the counter to a small control panel embedded in the wall. Keys in a quick code. The lights change. Not dimmed so much as altered.

The observation window is blacked out.

I sit up, slow.

Mekenna leans back against the counter. "And any

biotech with half a brain would keep track of said chips and would know where every last one of them was, and where they'd have no possibility of being."

The room is cold and so am I. "I'm not chipped. We don't even have medichips in Fane."

She shrugs, more with eyebrows then shoulders. "Perhaps. But perhaps you do. Or perhaps your father stole and repurposed one of ours. The Electorate will trust my word over his or even Arron's—the technology is mine, after all— and this whole charade is for *our* benefit. Now, perhaps that particular type of signature reader has a known tendency to fail when retesting subjects. Or perhaps your father is a conniving bastard who not only subverted our alliance but stole another man's child. Which would you prefer?"

She wants to change the story. My House in the balance and she doesn't even care.

And when it was Wren at stake, neither did I.

"Orrin," I say. "You want Orrin."

"So Arron *did* speak to you." Her smile eviscerates. "Yes, I want my husband back."

"No matter what? Even if it hurts?"

The smile crumbles in a ragged line. "He's dead, isn't he?"

"No, he's married."

Her expression doesn't change, caught as if the muscles broke.

"He has a restaurant and a ten-year-old. A boy. With freckles. I found an article in the feeds. Lord Westlet can show you."

I've gutted her. She's bleeding all over the sterile floor, and I don't have sealant enough to stop it and what I do have won't make it better.

But I offer it anyway.

"You don't need an ultimatum." I slide off the bed onto unsteady feet. "If you want to talk to Orrin, I'll make it happen. If you'd rather yell at Dad, I'll send him in. It doesn't have to be a game. You can just ask."

"THAT WAS AMAZING, DEAREST," SAYS MY MOTHER.

I freeze in the doorway between the lab and the lab's cluttered office.

Genevieve leans against the wall, a breezy tangle of flowers and salt. She peers past me and says, "Do pardon us, Mekenna," before closing the door.

The office is tiny, more an antechamber between the lab and the observation room—the door to which is also shut tight. I can't even hear muffled shouting now.

Which means they've moved past shouts to threats.

Genevieve's skirt brushes purple gloss against the stacked filecases as she lifts my hand and smooths the sealant with a gentle finger.

Or else the injected meds are kicking in.

"How ever did Gavin manage it?" she asks.

"He didn't."

"Now we both know that's not true." Airy and teasing.

"Then you know wrong." I yank free and pain spikes from my wrist to my heart. Or the other way around. I hug one to the other. "You don't get to hurt us by claiming me."

She bites her lip. "I would never—you're my daughter, Asa. I would never hurt you. You know that, right? You have to know that."

Me. That's me in her voice.

I shrink back but she eases closer.

"If Gavin hadn't locked me out, do you think I'd have missed a *second* of your growing up? That I wouldn't have loved to have shown you off? You were such a cute baby, small and perfect." She smooths my scalp with a touch even my bones feel, petal light and nail-edged. "And such lovely hair. This color suits you, but it's much too short. Gavin's idea, no doubt? Odd." Something flits across her lips and her eyes grow old. "He used to quite enjoy length. Never mind, dearest, we'll find a way to make it grow."

My hair will be short until I die.

Her hand slides down to my jaw. "Baby—"

"I'm not your baby!" I push away. "Or your darling or dearest or anything else."

"No, you're right. You're the Heir."

"I'm not—"

"To Galton," she says.

And my guts join Mekenna's on the floor. "What?"

"There was an accident, last year. Jaered cannot have more children." She takes a step, the hint of dewpetals in water. "He has no siblings. His mother had no siblings, nor his grandfather. You are the last of his line."

"No." I shake my head, block her out. "No."

"He will not give you up." Another step, gloss and thorns. "Nor should he. Ba—Asa, *this* is your inheritance. What you were born for. Nothing in Fane compares. Even your largest

281

city could fit within one of Annasan's lesser districts. And Westlet! Not that it doesn't have its share of charm mind you, but trees? In the capital? I've seen more birds' nests than people. Of course they have territory enough, and there's the blood bond to contend with, but you were made for grander things and we can make them happen."

Her hand falls on my heart.

I'll make it happen, I'd promised Mekenna. *I'll make it happen.*

"I. Am. Fane." I squeeze my fists until my wrist screams, and the truth blazes everywhere. "And nothing touches *that*."

Flame rises through her cheeks and chokes her eyes as she opens her mouth and—

Laughs. "Such *fire*, and you were such a little thing. How I've missed seeing you grow."

My heart smears with the red on my shirt.

"All of you, Wren and Emmaline. You can't image what it's like, being locked out. I'd forgive Gavin anything but that. If only he—"

The observation door opens and other voices soar in.

"—take your word on it?" asks Lord Galton, brutal tenor. "No, she comes with me."

"I haven't the slightest interest in your expectations," Lord Westlet nearly purrs. "The results are sent and cannot—what was it?—be 'deleted, overwritten, or tampered with.'"

"How incredibly *convenient*."

"Why, yes, the Electorate thought so. It was their idea."

Eagle fills the doorway, and our eyes meet. My chest knots in relief or joy or terror and all I want is to grab his hand and run.

He steps inside and shuts the rising argument out.

Genevieve swallows a sigh. "Eagle, is it? Looking for some quiet?"

He walks forward, focuses on me and me only. She might not exist. My heart kicks up.

"I'm quite sure it's loud enough out there to give anyone a headache, but if you don't mind, my daughter and I are—"

I reach out and he pulls me away from her and opens the lab door, stopping just inside.

"Mekenna," Eagle says, but his voice says, *out*.

Mekenna is still leaning against the steel counter, face stripped and dying.

"Let her alone," I say.

His hand tightens on the handle.

"Eagle, sweetheart," says Genevieve from behind. "As I said, we were in a—"

He spins, slides an arm over her shoulders and almost hauls her to the observation room door, which he magically opens to push her through. "My Lady," he says, stepping back.

"Really," she says, "I'm not sure—"

He slams the door in her face.

I nod to Mekenna and gently close her back in the lab. I turn and run into Eagle who is somehow right *here*, forearm leveraged on the door above my head.

"What happened? What did she say?" he asks, like the world ended and I didn't bother to tell him.

In the three seconds since I left the lab.

"God, Eagle, what *hasn't* happened?"

"I haven't killed anyone yet." Serious, almost austere, as if he's a vengeance ghost from one of Wren's favorite dramas, suited up and ready to go. I laugh. I can't help it. Big, silent bubbles I can't stop because every time I look at him they just bounce more.

His jaw sets and I'm half sure he'll launch into an epic ghostly monologue, except—the corner of his mouth upends on a lopsided smile.

The giggles fade. Catch on the half-moon scar that twines his mouth and turns it sneaky. The brown of his eyes echoes in his lips. Warmth and wonder like life is this shiny, beautiful thing.

No wonder he smiles so rarely. Everyone would forget how to breathe.

He kisses me. A series of kisses. Brief and gone and back again, until the seconds between are too many and too much and I follow his lips so he'll *stay*. And he does. Hand on my neck as mine finds his hair, and then we're out of sync and in rhythm. Upended or anchored or tangled or breaking, and his smile radiates under my skin.

Our noses brush, his eyes still closed. "I won't let them."

"Let them what?"

He presses his forehead to mine. "Take you to Galton. For retesting."

There's more, I can feel it, but his eyes don't open.

"And if I say no?" I say.

"They promise to take you. By force. *In* force."

Galton will invade.

"No!" I duck away from Eagle, run to the observation room door and pull it open.

The room centers on Galton and Dad. Dad's hand locked around the other's raised fist. Galton must have swung.

Galton bends so close to Dad, they could almost kiss. "You will hand her over. I don't know what armies you amassed during your lockdown, but I can promise—they won't be enough." Galton pulls free with an easy twist, as if Dad's hold was no barrier. Sees me in the doorway. Offers a mocking, half salute. "Next week, Daughter."

Not a threat or a promise. Those would assume the

possibility of doubt.

Galton holds out a hand to Genevieve. She takes his arm, but she watches Dad and Dad alone.

You idiot, she mouths.

And they're gone. A swish of heels and skirts disappearing into the hall. The room a vacuum in their wake.

Lord Westlet looks at the Lady, but her face is as etched as his.

She smooths her wrinkle-less dress. "I should—I should see them out."

Lord Westlet nods and leans against the observation window, waits for Dad to move.

Dad doesn't.

I can't, either.

Eagle's behind me, hand on my shoulder.

"The Electorate won't back Galton's lab over Mekenna's," Lord Westlet says at last. "He has ties here, but they are not *that* good. The second test would not have transmitted. Assuming Mekenna's silence, there's nothing to say it even happened."

"Yes," Dad's lips barely move. "But will they back me?"

"With force? I can't offer that." Dad's chin lifts, and Lord Westlet sighs. "If you cannot feed your people, you cannot fight a war and I cannot fight it for you. I haven't the soldiers or resources to face Galton alone. And should I be idiot enough to try, Daric will have the perfect excuse to rend this House from the inside." His words gain a bitter edge. "This alliance and your fuel was supposed to prevent that."

Dad nods. Accepts.

Everything.

"I need to talk to Dad," I tell Eagle.

Eagle shifts, fingers just brushing my neck as he steps past me through the door. "Father, a word?"

Lord Westlet turns toward us. "Now?"

"Yes."

The Lord shakes his head but pushes off the window and moves to the hall door. Eagle starts to follow.

"Wait." I reach for Eagle's jacket, check the pocket where he'd slipped Wren's digislate. It's still there. "I got the schematics, they're in the top level folder. Don't let him tell Dad about Emmie."

He doesn't quite smile and disappears after his dad. I wait until the door closes, then stand before mine.

"I'll go," I say.

Dad's head snaps up.

"Galton can't have more kids. Genevieve said there was an accident or something. It's not about the treaty. I don't think they care. So I'm going to go." The words come easy. No fight to get them out. "And no matter what Emmie says, you have to bring Wren here. The treatments are different

287

and Wren deserves the chance. Eagle will look after her. He's sorting out Lord Westlet now, so we'll have the food. So you just need to bring Wren. And let Mekenna yell at you, because that's your fault and you can't pretend it isn't. And—" Now the words do want to fight. "And you can't tell Eagle I'm going, because—just because."

Because he'll hate me. He won't forgive me.

Dad doesn't move, hasn't since I started.

"So you have to be there for Wren and Mekenna. And Eagle, if he needs you. And I know you'll watch over Emmie."

He looks at me. Just looks. I don't brace my feet and square my shoulders, or do anything much except look back.

Dad lifts his arm, pushes his sleeve off his communicator watch and taps the screen. As if any incoming missive or issued order is more important than this.

My wrist throbs and so do I. "Our tech won't work here, Dad. The feed protocols are different."

He doesn't even look up. "What did I do to Mekenna?"

"You trapped her husband in lockdown and now he's remarried with a kid."

The taps hesitate. "Ah. And where is she?"

"In the lab."

"I'll speak with her." He shakes out his sleeve and moves to the office door.

"And Wren?" I ask before he steps through. "You have

to look after Wren and Eagle. I won't be here, so it has to be you. I have your word?"

Dad meets my eyes, his face a map of every line already crossed.

"You don't have to worry, Asa," he says and closes the door.

FANE

THE LACERATED SEAMS ON EAGLE'S SHOULDER don't match up. Like his lacerated grunts when he tried to take his shirt off himself before letting me help. Dad is at the main complex, but Eagle wouldn't let me check his sealant anywhere but our tower, so we left.

Eagle sits sideways in the kitchen chair, right hand laced through its slatted back. Most of the kitchen is brushed steel, and the reflective table gleams under the scattered mess of gauze and sealant. I scoured our whole tower for medikits, from our bathrooms on the floor above to the docking bay below, and found three.

As if anything can fix the angry mess I made of Eagle's skin.

I rip a sealant packet, willing my right hand not to shake and my left fingers to work. The stupid acclimation process is taking forever, and now my whole left side doesn't want to function.

"You need meds," I say. "Real meds and stitches."

Soon. Tomorrow. So someone else will know to check him when I'm gone.

"I'm fine," he says, achy and exhausted.

"It'll *scar*."

"Whatever."

"Stop it, just—" The packet slips from my hand and skids across the tile. I'd kick it, but Eagle needs it so I can't.

Besides, it's under the table.

I bend, but my knees wobble and I crash to all fours.

"Asa?"

"Okay, I'm okay. Just dropping things." I crawl under the table.

The elevator pings and the opening doors swish in Lady Westlet's voice.

"The man is a marvel. If you're serious about transferring your daughter here, his medicenter is by far the best in the . . . *Eagle?*"

I scramble clear of the table as Eagle shoots from the chair, turning so his back faces away from the elevator, the Lady, and—

Dad.

"Mother," says a conversational Eagle, as if his bare chest isn't glinting in the overheads.

She matches his calm, adds disinterest. "What happened to your shoulder?"

"Nothing."

"Fascinating." The Lady's smile nearly blinds. "Because

that looked like something."

"He needs stitches." I push myself up and tilt into Eagle's vacated chair. Catch myself before I fall.

Eagle's at my side, hand on my arm.

"I'm fine," I say.

"No, you're not."

"Stitches."

"No, *explanation*," says the Lady with House-leveling patience.

Dad pales and marches toward Eagle. "When?"

"When what?" the Lady asks but Dad's *here*, one step away from Eagle and singeing the air.

"When did you chip her?" Dad asks.

"She's not chipped." Eagle doesn't budge.

Neither does Dad.

"It's fine," I say.

"If your body doesn't acclimate, it will shut down. Wren was on three sets of medications for a month. Have you had *any*?" He switches to Eagle. "Did you even give her the initiation pill, or did you just press *inject*?"

Now Eagle wobbles.

"I'm *fine*," I say.

And if I'm not, I'll be in Galton, so it won't matter.

"*When*?" Dad asks.

"About seven hours before the transport picked us up,"

Eagle answers, hoarse.

"Eagle!" I say.

Dad swears loud enough my teeth rattle. "If she dies from this, boy, I swear to God—"

"No, you *won't*." I push Dad back. "Your word, remember? Your *word*."

"Of course Asa isn't chipped. We have the scan." Lady Westlet steps into our ever-tightening circle, long skirt bunching against the chair. "Can we please discuss something relevant? Like, say, my son's shoulder?"

"That is exactly what we *are* discussing, my Lady," Dad says.

"Oh, yes? Then please, enlighten me."

"Because they dug his out. Where else would they get one?"

She draws herself up. "If you think I'd let Mekenna put any of her highly experimental tech into *my* sons, you are much—"

"They chipped me in the meteor storm," says Eagle. "That's why I survived."

Her expression keeps its steel, but her hand clamps onto the chair. "You're chipped?"

"Was."

"Was. Yes. *Explain*. Why—?"

"To subvert the damn test, why else?" Dad lays both

hands on the table, as if he wants to throw them up. "She needs the med regimen. Can you get that?"

The steel slips. "You mean, she's really—?"

He rounds on her. "Asa is *Fane*. And seeing as she saved your precious blood bond, might you at least find her the damn meds?"

"IT MIGHT NOT SCAR." MY HAND HOVERS OVER HIS shoulder, air-traces the Lady's even, perfect stitches. She found me pills—a whole handful, plus two injections—and a pain-numbing agent for Eagle. He slumps now, instead of being coiled tight. The cuts seem smoother, less angry, but that could just be the way the gold light bounces. We're in the living room now. "Everything matches up."

"Feel better?"

I stick out my tongue. Not that he sees. "Yes."

"But do you?" He leans back into the couch. "Feel better?"

"I think so." Some of the numb bits tingle.

"You sure?" Eagle takes my left hand and spreads fingers, scanning each like they'll fall apart. His thumb finds the center of my palm. "Do you feel this?"

A little. Sort of. My soul does.

"Can you close your hand?"

I try. The fingers curl some. Not enough apparently, because his eyebrows bunch over his nose. I slide my hand away to open his waxy palm instead.

"You know, I was thinking, without your medichip, you can get a new hand. Some are really amazing. There's this one that has thirty-six thousand contact points you can dial up or down—so if you want to feel the difference between tepid and lukewarm, or hold an active blastshard, you can."

"An active blastshard."

I shrug. "You never know. We could go look, you could try it."

And if he likes it, he could order one or have it custom built. Maybe this time the medics would get the color right. Maybe I'd get the chance to see it.

He straightens. "Asa?"

"Yeah?"

His fingers slide up to my needle-chewed wrist, and I can't tell if he's checking the bandage or sifting through the thoughts in his head. "You said you'd take it back."

"What?"

"On Urnath, you said you'd take it back."

Oh.

I try to sink away, but he holds fast. "I wouldn't. Take it back. Or let Galton take you. I won't. I love you."

He searches my face, thirty-six thousand contact points between his eyes and my heart, rooting me inside and out.

It's not real. I swear I started with the truth, but now it's stuck in incandescence and the perfect lines of his perfect mouth. The sunshine glows when the world ends and there's nothing left to do but whatever you can.

Which I do. Have. Will.

I break apart.

"Asa?" His hands rise to my neck and cheeks and I can

feel them, every brush. "God, Asa, I'm sorry. You don't have to—"

"I love you." Ragged and teary. "I love you like everything."

Confusion catches in his hesitant smile. "And that's bad?"

"No! Never." I wipe my face, smear tears all over my crinkled sleeves. "I mean, do you want to go look at those hands tomorrow? We could go to the city, just us. Buy some icelees and puffcakes and—"

"Galton won't invade." Eagle cups my face. "We'll figure it out."

"I know."

"We *will*."

"I know."

But I'm not convincing enough, and he leans in until our eyes level. "Asa—"

I kiss him. Taste my name on his tongue, or maybe my heart. Cover his hands with mine and offer every truth in me, broken and mended, so he won't need convincing, he'll *know*.

"I love you," I say, more shape then sound. "Don't forget."

I HOLD WREN'S HAND AS WE WALK THROUGH HER new ward. I walk. She floats on her meditransport hoverbed. Dad strides ahead with Medic Harwick, the lead specialist assigned to her care. He's short and plump with rapid fire answers to every question—even ones we didn't ask. He seems fascinated by Wren's case, or rather, Suzanna's case.

We said she is a distant family cousin—which should give her priority care without making her a target if someone has a vendetta against Dad.

I didn't think he would fly her here so fast. It's nice. I can finish the story we were reading.

Westlet medicenters don't do themes, but they do have windows. The whole outer wall is a spotless pane through which the trees glow sunset gold. The sun catches Wren, too. Smooths the starburst of her scalp.

"Here we are." Medic Harwick stops outside an open door at the end of the corridor, wide enough to accommodate a hoverbed and a half. "If you don't mind, m'lady, I'll take over from here. Give us a couple hours to run some tests, and we'll have her ready and waiting."

I nod and he smiles, takes my place at Wren's side. Guides her through into a blur of green-coated medics and paisley walls, and closes the door.

"This is nice," I say. "She'll like it."

Dad considers the checkered ceiling, the cheery bustle, me. "This is a long shot. You know that."

"I know."

And I do.

Dad nods, gestures down the hall. "Shall we?"

We retrace our steps back to the alcoved waiting room—a glass box stitched into the building, with blue rugs and puffed white chairs that seems to float over tree-lined streets.

We sit side by side. Watch the hanging newsfeed screen in the corner, where Finch and Dravers mouth silent arguments transcribed by scrolling white text. Nothing about my blood test or Galton. Eagle says with me proven as Fane, it's in the Electorate's best interest to pretend it never happened. Mekenna erased the inconclusive result, and no one seems to know.

But then, it's only been a day and a half.

The hall fills with footsteps and laughter, and I crane to see where it comes from.

Eagle should be here soon. He is at the loading dock making sure Lord Westlet follows through with the promised shipments so Dad can help me with Wren.

More footsteps. Harried medics, a few visitors, but no one in a hood.

"It'll take him another half hour at least," Dad says.

"Right." I face front, hands in my lap.

Dad watches the screen. "You two get on, then? Off camera?"

"He's pretty wonderful."

"And have I him to thank for the food, or you?"

I shrug. "Both?"

He nods. "Are the meds working?"

"I think so." I wiggle my left fingers. They're slow and sluggish, but better. Like my back and side. "I should be ready for—I'll be ready."

Another nod. People pass. Dravers punctuates points with long nails.

"Eagle's hand glitches," I say. "I'm afraid he won't get a new one unless someone bugs him about it."

Dad doesn't say anything.

"And Emmie. I'd like to see her. Before I go."

He brushes off his slacks and stands. "Coffee?"

I rub my sore wrist. "Okay."

Heads turn as he strides through the windowed corridor. Maybe they know him, but more likely they just *sense* him. When he rounds the corner, there's nothing to watch but trees and Finch's bushy eyebrows. They crease and bounce, dance a jig and—flatline. His whole face flatlines. So does Dravers. It might be a glitch in the feeds, except Dravers raises a jerky hand to her mouth and smears her lipstick.

They know. About the second test. They know.

I brace both arms on my seat.

Finch flattens his hands on the table, takes forever to look up. The captions kick in.

Forgive us, we've just received word. It appears Lord Jaered of Galton died last night, due to a heart attack. We have no further information as yet, but should know more within the hour.

Dead?

Galton can't be dead, he was fine. More than fine. He faced Dad down and *won*.

And after Dad lost, when it was just him and me, Dad said something.

The caption scrolls with speed, full of speculation and commentary. Lord Jaered has no direct Heir. The House will be in stasis while they scramble back generations to find one. No decisions will be made or permanent orders issued. Galton is in an effective political lockdown.

Which means every distant branch of the Galton House family has a shot at the Lordship, assuming they can produce a viable Heir. Even if Genevieve still claimed me as Jaered's, no one would back her without proof—and probably not even then. Why give me the House when it could be theirs? Genevieve isn't blood, her title depended on Jaered's.

And after Jaered left, when it was just me and Dad, Dad said something he has *never* said to me before. Not once. Not even in quarantine, because Dad doesn't make promises he can't keep.

Heavy tread. Gleaming black shoes and gray slacks. Dad stands at my shoulder, two green mugs in his work-worn hands.

He holds out a cup. I take it automatically, with fingers that somehow work. He reclaims his seat, glances at the screen then looks at me.

You don't have to worry, Asa.

"Drink your coffee," Dad says.

I hold the mug in my lap. He stares out the window. I slip one hand onto the armrest nearest him. Open, palm up.

His inches, hovers, covers mine. His palm is bigger, knuckles wider and fingers shorter, but not enough to notice.

He still has Wren's hands.

And mine.

ACKNOWLEDGMENTS

Mom, who defines heart.

Victoria Marini, who breathes magic.

Lisa Cheng, who voices depth.

Janet Johnson, who paints perfection in exclamation points.

Lisha Cauthen, who brightens the world in gifs.

Seabrooke Leckie, who helped save the title.

Sarah Belliston, who totally got gypped on kisses.

Sofia Embid, who sorted through the confusion.

Louise Hawes, who inspires our best.

Jessica Spotswood, who saw Asa's strength.

Kathleen Duey, who asked the perfect question.

The Mainely Writing crew, who weave mornings in quiet.

The Tuesday group, who knit evenings in laughter.

And to everyone who read my work and helped me grow—

You are in my thoughts and heart.